The Convent

Also by Panos Karnezis

Little Infamies
The Maze
The Birthday Party

The Convent

PANOS KARNEZIS

W. W. NORTON & COMPANY
New York • London

For information about special discounts for
bulk purchases, please contact W. W. Norton Special Sales at
specialsales@wwnorton.com or 800-233-4830

Manufacturing by Courier Westford
Production manager: Anna Oler

Library of Congress Cataloging-in-Publication Data

Karnezis, Panos, 1967–
The convent / Panos Karnezis. — 1st American ed.
p. cm.
ISBN 978-0-393-05699-0 (hardcover)
1. Convents—Spain—Fiction. 2. Nuns—Spain—Fiction.
3. Foundlings—Fiction. 4. Life change events—Fiction. I. Title.
PR6111.A76C66 2010b
823'.92—dc22

W. W. Norton & Company, Inc.,
500 Fifth Avenue, New York, N.Y. 10110
www.wwnorton.com

W. W. Norton & Company Ltd., Castle House,
75/76 Wells Street, London W1T 3QT

1 2 3 4 5 6 7 8 9 0

The Convent

Those whom God wishes to destroy he first makes mad. Sister Lucía, the young novice, was late leaving for the city and in her hurry to get to the car did not notice the old suitcase until she had reached the bottom of the steps. It was a leather suitcase with brass corners, a wooden handle and locks covered with rust, while on its lid, which bore the signs of an unhappy life spent travelling the world, someone had cut several big round holes. At first she thought that it would be full of clothes for the poor, which people often donated to the convent, but when she looked through a hole she was so terrified by what she saw that she let out a cry and ran back inside.

At that time Sister María Inés, mother superior of the convent of Our Lady of Mercy, had finished her correspondence and sat at her desk with her eyes shut to purge her mind of mundane thoughts. Even on a bright day like this the windows barely let enough light into the room, which was both her office and living quarters. In one corner were a narrow bed with a very thin mattress and a small table with a burning vigil lamp. Several religious icons hung on the wall among patches of crumbling plaster, while in a niche stood a statue of a praying Virgin. The rest of the room was filled with chairs, armoires and other pieces of furniture that served no practical purpose: Sister María Inés had few belongings and even fewer visitors. When the young novice walked into the room the Mother Superior opened her eyes and looked at her with disappointment.

Sometimes she wished that she were with the Carthusians so that she would not have to speak. She had tried to make her nuns commit themselves to solitude and silence, but had been less successful than she would have liked. She had taken her own vows at the turn of the century, before the advent of the telephone and the radio, when it had been easier to lead a life devoted to God. Since then she had witnessed life becoming less calm and contemplative even there in the convent, despite the fact that their only means of communication with the outside world was the weekly trip by car to the city many miles away. Sister María Inés was the first to admit the benefits of progress, but she still believed that humankind had been given perhaps more intelligence than was necessary. With only a hint of reproach, she acknowledged the young novice and asked: 'Is it the Wandering Jew again, Lucía?'

In the past year the girl had claimed to have seen him five times, and had rushed to ring the bell in the chapel. She had been mistaken on every occasion. They had turned out to be solitary hunters who had lost their way in the sierra or intrepid gypsies who had come to sell the nuns merchandise that no one wanted to buy in the city. The girl shook her head: it was not the Wandering Jew. Sister María Inés came to the window and looked at the bottom of the steps. A moment later she was there. She opened the locks of the old suitcase, raised the lid with a trembling hand and saw a baby lying naked on a thick layer of cotton wool that was damp with sweat, for the big holes in the lid had allowed the baby to breathe but not relieved him from the late-summer heat. It was a boy. His umbilical cord had been cut carelessly and the shrivelled piece hung down from his belly like a deflated balloon. Despite the heat and the blazing sun, he was asleep and did not even wake up when Sister María Inés lifted him out of the suitcase and carried him to her room, followed by the young novice. She wrapped the child in a clean towel and laid him on her bed. Then she said: 'Tell me what happened.'

'I was on my way to the car,' the nun said. 'The suitcase was at the bottom of the steps, Reverend Mother. I didn't touch it.'

Sister María Inés had taught the novice to drive after Sister Beatriz, the nun responsible for driving to the city once a week, had asked to be excused from that duty. For the past month it was Sister Lucía who travelled on the road to the city more than thirty miles away to buy provisions, collect the post and keep the nuns up to date with the latest gossip. Their car, a very old Model T Ford with a retractable roof and acetylene headlights, used to belong to the Bishop, who had donated it to the convent after buying a new one.

The Mother Superior asked: 'Did you see anyone leaving the child there?'

'No, Reverend Mother.'

'Who else knows?'

'No one. I came straight to you.'

The Mother Superior observed the child for a moment, still unable to believe what she saw, and then dismissed the novice with a strict tone of voice: 'Now go. And I will decide when to tell the sisters.'

When she was alone, she sat on the edge of the bed and continued to watch the sleeping baby in silence. This was one of the rare occasions in her life when she did not know what to do. She had joined the convent of Our Lady of Mercy a year after the man she wanted to marry had died in a place on the other side of the world, and had never doubted that she had made the right decision. His portrait, in white uniform, hung on the wall among the grave faces of the saints, who seemed to look at her with disapproval. She knew it verged on blasphemy, but she did not take it down even when the Bishop visited the convent to celebrate Mass with the nuns one Sunday a month. He did not mind: apart from that little lapse, Sister María Inés was an excellent servant of God. She wore the same habit as the day that she had taken her vows, and it was still in good condition, with some commendable wear at the knees after years of daily prayers. Under it she wore a simple loose garment, which neither kept her warm in winter nor cool in the summer, but protected her soul from the temptations of vanity. The soft leather soles of her shoes allowed her to appear in a room as if out of nowhere, a skill that always surprised her nuns and made Sister Lucía think of her as a closet saint with preternatural powers.

After staring at the child for a long time, Sister María Inés emerged from her contemplation and became herself again. The first thing that she had to take care of was his food. She went to the kitchen, where the nuns were preparing lunch, and asked for boiled milk, cream and sugar. The women were intrigued: Sister María Inés always warned them that eating between meals was the first step on the path to gluttony. But when they dared to ask her about the food, she silenced them with only a few words: 'Nothing that should concern you at the moment. I will make an announcement after vespers.'

Back in her room, she mixed in a bowl a little of the milk with some of the cream and sugar, thinned the mixture down with water and added, with good sense, a few drops of cod-liver oil to fortify the newborn's delicate health. Then she took him in her arms and began to feed him. She had never given birth herself but knew how to look after children and the sick. After she had taken her vows, she had asked to be posted in Africa, where she had spent three years in a mission hospital. She had begun as an untrained nurse, but in her spare time had studied the principles of medicine and become indispensable to the doctors. It had been gratifying work, and perhaps she would have been there still if the unexpected consequences of a malaria attack had not forced her to return to Europe at a time when Africa was starting to feel like home to her.

When she finished feeding the child, she held him against her chest and patted his back until he brought up wind. Then she put him on the bed to sleep and turned her attention to the suitcase. She examined its old locks, the lining made of the kind of cotton wool that could be bought in any pharmacy, the holes in the lid that had been cut as if the child's life depended on them, but found no clues to the mystery. Whoever had left the suitcase on the steps of the convent had planned it well, and Sister María Inés thought with leniency that if perhaps that person had not loved the child enough to keep him, he or she at least cared that he survived.

The bell began to ring, and she considered quickly what to do. In all her years in the convent she had never missed prayers. She looked at the child for a moment and, satisfied that he would stay asleep for a while, she decided to go. She made sure that the sunlight through the windows would not fall on him, and walked softly away so as not to wake him up. When she opened the door, she came face to face with Sister Beatriz. The nun blushed.

'What are you doing here?' Sister María Inés asked.

'I was on my way to the chapel. I stopped to remind you that it is time for prayer. Did you hear the bell?'

Sister María Inés looked at her with reproach. She said: 'My ears are big enough. I do not need to be reminded. I have no intention of failing in my duties for as long as I can walk.' She closed the door behind her softly and walked towards the stairs. She said: 'I am glad you are joining us in prayer.'

'I apologise.'

'A nun is not a nun unless she prays regularly.'

'I prayed in my room, Reverend Mother.'

'In your room,' Sister María Inés repeated. 'I am pleased to hear it.'

When Sister Beatriz had come to the convent, a few years

earlier, it was not to join the Order but to escape the terrible influenza epidemic that had spread across the world, killing in one year more people than the Black Death in the Middle Ages and even more than the Great War. The Mother Superior had been impressed by the young woman's humility and diligence. So when her parents later died in the epidemic, Sister María Inés suggested that she take the veil. The young woman had agreed. The next time that the priest visited the convent, the Mother Superior spoke to him. At the end of the Mass, he called the girl to the altar and asked her whether she was willing to die to the world, renounce all pomp and vanities and put on the habit of the sisters. To all these questions the young woman had answered affirmatively, and rising from the altar steps she walked down the aisle and out of the chapel to receive her habit. She had reappeared wearing the white dress and veil of a novice, and after repeating her vow she had been given the name by which she was to be known ever since: Beatriz.

Two years later she had knelt before the priest again and taken her permanent vows. Sister María Inés had no reason to fear that the young woman would turn out to be anything but an exemplary nun. Sister Beatriz carried out her duties with great enthusiasm, and if she ever missed prayers the Mother Superior blamed it on the religious zeal with which all her nuns committed themselves to their duties and the practice of fasting. She often reproached them for not taking care of themselves and indulging in meaningless mortification of the flesh, which made them pass out during prayers and drop to the chapel floor. Then Sister María Inés had to interrupt the service and give them a sniff of smelling salts to bring them round.

The two women went downstairs and crossed the cloistered courtyard towards the chapel. The clock on the bell tower showed five minutes past midday. The Mother Superior quickened her pace, and Sister Beatriz followed behind. In the chapel the other nuns sat on the pews waiting. When the small congregation heard the two women, they turned round and stared at the door. Sister María Inés lifted her habit and climbed the steps to the chapel with a stern expression. At the door she stopped to dip a finger in the stoup and cross herself.

'I apologise,' she said, entering the chapel and looking straight ahead. 'Sister Beatriz delayed me.'

Without slowing down, she took her place at the altar and began the oration: '*Deus in adjutorium meum intende.*' The nuns stood up and responded, crossing themselves: '*Domine ad adjuvandum me festina.*' Sister María Inés was usually pleased to be in the cool, dark chapel, where the nuns assembled eight times a day to pray, but today she felt with shame that she could not concentrate. Nevertheless, she had stood at the altar long enough to be able to carry out her duties without anyone noticing that her mind was on other things. Hoping that God would forgive her this rare moment of weakness, she put on her glasses, took a breath that seemed to rise from the bottom of her soul and opened the medieval lectionary. The lesson that day was from Genesis. She read the long sentences in a clear and confident voice, without drawing breath, which was another of her frightful supernatural skills, and only when she finished and breathed again, calm and commanding and satisfied with her performance, did she realise that she had read the wrong passage. She shut the heavy book and stared at her congregation. Even though no one said anything, she felt miserable about her mistake. But she could not stop thinking of that morning's extraordinary event. Gradually the smell of candle wax helped her to concentrate. She was about to begin another hymn when a distant sound travelled into the chapel and ruled out any chance of ending the prayer in peace. It was a sound that had never before been heard within the walls of the old convent, but in the solemn silence it was impossible to mistake it for anything less terrifying than what it was: the gentle sound of a baby crying.

Time had given the convent of Our Lady of Mercy a mystical appearance. Built in the sixteenth century as a place of calm and contemplation, it stood on top of a hill in an otherwise uninhabited part of the sierra among dense pine forest. In the middle of the convent was a big courtyard with a splendid cloister of pointed arches and twisted columns. On one side of the courtyard was the chapel with its tall bell tower, where in the nineteenth century a clock held by two stone angels had been installed with money given by a widowed merchant in memory of his wife. The interior of the chapel was decorated with beautiful but now faded frescoes that depicted the Stations of the Cross. On the other sides of the courtyard, connected via the cloister, which offered a sheltered passage from the elements, were the Mother Superior's house, the dormitory for the nuns and the refectory, where the nuns assembled after vespers for recreation until the bell rang for night prayer.

Also facing the courtyard was the old school for novices, which had not been used in many years and had been left to stand derelict. These days the only novice in the convent was Sister Lucía, whom the Mother Superior taught in her office. Lucía participated in the full canonical hours and spent the morning reading the scriptures, while the other nuns busied themselves with the upkeep of the convent. The Mother Superior taught her Latin, set her spiritual exercises and tests of humility, heard her confession and gave her Holy Communion against the rules of the Church: only a priest could do that. When she was not taking instruction, the young novice made competent embroideries of religious subjects, which added to the modest income of the convent. In the afternoons the Mother Superior took her for long walks in the orchard, and they discussed the creation of the world, how many nails were used to crucify Christ and other important doctrinal matters in between brief rests in the shade to admire the beauty of nature. Sister Lucía paid attention to the older woman, asked questions of elaboration rather than disbelief and memorised everything. Although she was not very bright, she was pious, and the Mother Superior, who had guided many girls through the noviciate, had no doubt that one day Lucía would enter the kingdom of Heaven.

The guesthouse behind the old school for novices was rarely used, but was kept in good order by the nuns, who prided themselves on their hospitality. It was here the Bishop had slept on the few occasions that he had stayed the night during his monthly visits. Tempted by the splendid mountain views from the balcony, he would sit with a glass of cold lemonade to watch the sun disappear below the pine trees and make small talk with the Mother Superior, their discussion punctuated by the calls of the wise owls living in the roofs of the convent.

A corridor from the refectory led to the kitchen, the bakehouse and the buttery, where the provisions brought by car from the city were kept: sacks of flour, pulses and grains, barrels of salted fish, an icebox made of wood and insulated with cork for those rare occasions when they bought fresh fish.

Every morning, at five o'clock, the sound of the bell woke the nuns, and the first thing they did was to kneel before their beds and pray for the suffering of humankind. Then they washed, dressed and hurried to the chapel, where the Mother Superior was ready to start the dawn prayer. They had time for tea with a slice of bread and a piece of fruit in the refectory before they made their way back to the chapel for the office of prime. After the prayer they assembled in the courtyard, where the Mother Superior allocated them their tasks for the day. The women received their instructions with a bow and went to their posts in silence.

Every three hours they broke off to return to the chapel and pray. Before lunchtime Sister María Inés did her round of the convent to inspect their work. With her hands clasped under the sleeves of her habit, she asked questions, helped solve problems and was generous with her praise, but did not leave without reminding the women that the continuing existence of the convent as well as the salvation of their souls depended on the quality of their work. At one o'clock, they ate lunch without speaking to each other, while a sister read aloud from a book of prayers. Afterwards they had a little free time to write letters to relatives and do odd jobs for themselves.

After the mid-afternoon prayer, they resumed their work until it was time to assemble for supper, which began with each nun having a reluctant spoonful of that cod-liver oil. It was a practice started by the Mother Superior, who was aware of its health benefits from her missionary days. When supper finished, they had an hour of recreation, which they spent doing needlework, reading or, once a month, watching the magic lantern show which the Mother Superior would put on in the refectory with slides ordered by post. It was followed by vespers, and then the nuns were free until the night prayer and the Great Silence. In the middle of the night they left their beds to attend nocturns.

On the eastern transept of the chapel was the library, filled with religious manuscripts and printed books that had not been banned by the Inquisition. There were two gardens in the convent, one where the nuns grew the vegetables and herbs they used in the kitchen and one for the flowers they sold in the summer to a florist in the city to supplement their income. Behind the chapel was a well-equipped carpentry workshop, which had not been used in years, and a cemetery with crosses and gravestones covered with yellow moss where the nuns were buried. There were several other buildings and rooms in the convent, but like the school for novices they, too, had been left empty for a long time and had fallen into disrepair. The music room, where in the past the choir that was famous beyond the borders of the diocese practised, was now used for the storage of furniture and tools which no one wanted to admit that they would never use again. A group of white storks had made their nests on the tall chimneys of the convent, where they stayed until late October, and then left for the African coast, not to return until spring. Over the years the number of nuns in the convent had declined, and these days there were only five and the Mother Superior. Sister María Inés had no doubt that they were the last survivors of an age that was coming to its end.

When the nuns in the chapel heard the baby crying, they crossed themselves and looked at each other with terror. The Mother Superior spoke in a calm firm voice. 'Sister Carlota,' she said. Go to my room and feed the child. The milk is on the bedside table.' She gestured to the other nuns to stand and added: 'I will be with you as soon as we finish our prayer.'

Sister Carlota obeyed with a bow. She was the oldest nun in the convent, already old when Sister María Inés had arrived, but still carried out her daily tasks with a spirit that could only be understood as a candid contract with death not to call her over as long as she could be useful. The Mother Superior depended on her. Having been brought up in another time, Sister Carlota always carried out any instruction she was given, even if she disagreed with it. She was the one who had welcomed Sister María Inés when she had come back from Africa, and had taken her under her wing with maternal affection. They had remained close until Sister María Inés, having been elected mother superior, had reluctantly distanced herself from the old woman, convinced that their intimacy would compromise her authority.

The nuns watched Sister Carlota leave the chapel and turned to the Mother Superior. They did not dare ask her about the baby. Sister María Inés cleared her throat and resumed the service. The hymns did not dissolve the sense of mystery. She ordered the door shut, but she could tell that the nuns continued not to pay attention. When at last the prayers ended, the women remained on their pews with the hope of learning why there was a baby in the convent. But the Mother Superior was in no mood to explain. She said: 'That is it. Go in the peace of Christ.'

She left the chapel before them and hurried to her room. Sister Carlota was sitting on the bed with the child in her arms. He was no longer crying. The Mother Superior took him from her with great care and noticed a little silver medal pinned to the bed sheet with which the baby was wrapped.

'It is Santa Brígida,' Sister Carlota said. 'She will look after him.'

The sun had passed its highest point and slanted through the narrow windows. The heat in the room rose. On warm days like this, Sister María Inés often took refuge in the library, whose high-beam ceiling kept it cool all afternoon and allowed her to work there all day, emerging only for prayers and meals. But a room heavy with the smell of old parchment would not have been healthy for a newborn baby. Without taking her eyes from the child, she asked Sister Carlota to open a window. 'Only one,' she said.

The old nun did as she was told. She had a natural love of the young and defenceless. The mission closest to her heart was saving the stray dogs of the city and bringing them to the convent, where she cared for them as if she were Saint Francis of Assisi. Time had shown no mercy to her eyesight, but this did not prevent her from going about the convent at any time of day, for she knew the location of every room, staircase and corridor by heart. The Mother Superior said: 'The baby will need to be changed soon, Carlota. Make him some nappies from the softest cloth you can find.'

The nun promised that she would do so, and asked: 'Have you decided what to do with him, Reverend Mother?'

Sister María Inés shook her head.

'Perhaps someone would know of a childless couple,' the old nun suggested.

'That would be against the law,' the Mother Superior said.

'Then we could try the orphanage.'

The Mother Superior also dismissed that suggestion with a grimace. 'It would be like giving the baby away to the gypsies,' she said, and sent the nun away. 'I am sorry I made you miss the prayer, Carlota. The nappies and nothing else. I relieve you of your other duties for the rest of the day. Pray in your room.'

The old woman thanked her with a bow and left after giving the baby a lingering look. The Mother Superior rocked the child to sleep. No one was allowed in her room without her permission. She cleaned it with a care and commitment that one who did not know her might mistake for humility, but which was in fact a desire for privacy that despite her many years of convent life was as strong as ever. Every day she would wake up long before the bell summoned the sisters to the chapel for the dawn prayer, wash, put on her old habit and take a walk round the convent in the dark as quietly as a ghost, breathing in the night moisture redolent with the scent of pine in the air. Then she would unlock the door of the chapel, light the oil lamps that had gone off during the night, inspect the traps baited with chocolate and throw away the dead rats before Sister Carlota saw them and burst into tears.

By the time that dawn would break, she would be back in her room and sitting at her desk. Her administrative duties usually took up most of her morning. She prepared and signed invoices and recorded all transactions in a book filled with her beautiful handwriting, which she had learned from the medieval calligraphy manuals kept in the library. The convent had no bank account. She kept the money, the promissory notes from their various debtors and the ancient titles to the land that belonged to the convent from the days of King Philip II in a big coffer with three padlocks whose heavy keys hung with the rosary looped over her belt. After updating the accounts, she answered the many letters from women who enquired about taking the veil, trying not to discourage any from joining the convent but stressing the sacrifices that they should be prepared to make. Above all, she tried to estimate the intensity of their faith, for she knew that it was a decision invariably made on impulse, and urged them to take time to consider with great care what they were about to do. This she did perhaps too well because very few women ever wrote to her again.

Her afternoons were devoted to her favourite pastime: servicing the car. Like nursing, it was another skill that she had learned during her time in Africa. The old Ford was kept in a shed behind the chapel, where Midas, their superannuated donkey, also quietly lived out his twilight years. After lunch Sister María Inés put on a loose white smock over her habit and went to the shed where she pumped up the tyres of the car, topped up the radiator, lubricated the engine and fought the doomed fight against the rust that spread on its chassis. Once a month she polished the car from end to end with the wax the nuns used on the wooden floors of the convent. She did all the repairs herself, pleased that she saved the convent the money they would otherwise have to pay the mechanic in the city. She had begun to teach Sister Beatriz about car engines with the hope that one day she would take up the responsibility of keeping the Ford alive.

She would stay in the shed for a long time, breaking only for a brief meditation and the rosary. Then she would return to her room, hang up her smock and make her way to the chapel ahead of the sisters to prepare for the mid-afternoon prayer. She would walk up and down the nave carrying out her tasks in silent meditation, while the draught from the door would make the candles flicker and her shadow flutter on every wall. It was an important ritual. By the time the nuns would come in for the prayer, she would already be in the presence of the Holy Spirit.

But she did not go to the shed this afternoon. Rocking the baby to sleep, she stood at the window and looked at the steps where the suitcase had been found earlier that day. Sister Lucía had driven to the city and would not be back until after vespers. Sister María Inés went from window to window pulling the curtains. In the stifling room she began to sweat, and it was then with the baby in her arms that she understood the significance of what had happened that morning. She kissed the child on the forehead and looked at him as if his face were familiar to her. Then she said: 'It has been a very long time. I no longer expected you to come. But Our Lord behaves in ways that surprise even his most devoted servants.' When she was young, she had prayed to God for any sign of mercy, and had continued to pray for mercy for several years after becoming a nun, but He had not seemed to listen. Eventually she had given up praying for mercy, without admitting to herself that she was disappointed in God. Many more years had passed before she had asked His forgiveness for having doubted His wisdom, and still she would sometimes weep in bed with bursts of tears that were heard as far as the nuns' dormitory.

The baby had fallen asleep and she placed him on the bed. Then she went and put the old suitcase in the back of her wardrobe, and knelt in front of the statue of the Virgin to pray to the glory of God.

In the refectory the three nuns were cutting and parcelling the altar breads, their main source of income. The breads had to be ready before the women went to bed. Once a week, very early in the morning, a baker came from the city in a van to collect them. The nuns had spent the entire afternoon talking about the child and had fallen behind with their work. Now it was almost evening, and they worked in a hurry, no longer talking to each other. When Sister Carlota entered, they looked at her with expectation. Without saying a word, she went to the storeroom and came back with a clean tablecloth and the scissors. She sat at the table and began to cut the cloth in squares. Sister Teresa could not stand her silence. She asked: 'Have you learned anything about the baby?'

The old woman shrugged. 'I am not allowed to say. Ask the Mother. But I don't think she knows much either.'

The nuns resumed their work, but it was not long before Sister Ana spoke up. 'Nevertheless, he is here now. And we have to decide what to do.'

Sister Carlota cut another square from the tablecloth. She said: 'I think she means to keep him,' and put the piece of cloth with the ones she had already cut.

Sister Ana frowned. 'That is out of the question,' she said, and the lines on her face which owed more to her forbidding temperament than old age, deepened. She had come to the convent of Our Lady of Mercy from another convent, which she had left with bitterness because her abilities had not been fully acknowledged. She knew stenography, spoke German, French and Italian, and had brought with her a Remington typewriter made in the previous century and almost too heavy to lift, which only she could use. Sister María Inés did not like her but admired her clerical skills. She often asked her to help with her correspondence, even though she had ambivalent feelings towards the typewriter, which she suspected was invented to make lying easier. Her reasoning was simple: she believed that handwriting revealed the truth behind one's words no matter how hard one tried to hide it with subterfuges, ambiguities and outright lies. It was her opinion as an amateur graphologist. In fact she claimed that she could open any manuscript from the convent library and tell from the penmanship whether the medieval copyist had been a pious Christian or a lost soul who now burned in Hell.

Sister Ana had nothing but scorn for her theories but never dared say so in her presence. She cut another altar bread and said: 'I propose we discuss the matter of the child tonight.'

'There is no point,' Sister Beatriz said. 'The Mother makes her own decisions.'

'Not if she intends to keep the child. That would be a gross violation of the rules of this place.'

'The Mother knows the rules as well as you do. We'll have to abide by her decision.'

'Don't talk to me about obedience,' Sister Ana said and returned to her work. But it was not long before she spoke again: 'In any case there are higher authorities than the Mother in this world. I hope she intends at least to notify the Guardia.'

'There is also the Bishop,' Sister Carlota said.

At one end of the room, a large wooden Jesus on the Cross was fixed to the floor. The light cast his shadow on the wall as high up as the ceiling. After four centuries in the damp air of the convent, his body had turned a dull, almost black colour. The remains of a red colour on his crown of thorns were in fact real blood: some time in the eighteenth century, a mother superior had taken it down and worn it on Holy Week to recreate the Passion. It was one of those extravagances that Sister María Inés did not approve of because they seemed to her grim ailments of the soul rather than examples of great piety.

Sister Ana pointed at the old nun and said: 'Sister Carlota is right. His Excellency ought to know.'

'That is one thing we don't have to worry about,' Sister Teresa said. 'His Excellency is omniscient.'

Sister Ana shot her an angry glance. 'That is vulgarity. Sister Teresa, you ought to be ashamed of yourself.'

'It is the truth. The Bishop knows everything that goes on in here. He must have a crystal ball on his desk.'

'You are expected to obey His Excellency, Sister Teresa,' Sister Ana said.

Sister Carlota cut the last square from the tablecloth. 'Our vows are to God,' she said, inspecting her work.

Sister Teresa said: 'Exactly – not to Sister Ana.'

It was a calculated insult. From the day Sister Ana had taken her vows, more than a decade earlier, she had dreamed of being in charge of a convent, which she would make the leading one in the country. She hoped to fulfil her ambition in the convent of Our Lady of Mercy, where she had immediately taken on many responsibilities with a zeal that had impressed everyone. One of her first accomplishments had been the digging of an artesian well so that they could irrigate the crops without the need for a pump. Next she taught herself stenography and book-keeping, and asked permission to buy a gramophone, not in order to play music but to learn foreign languages by listening to records made for that purpose. All this she did without neglecting her religious duties. She never missed prayers; she worked in the kitchen, said the rosary, did her penances and everything else that was expected of her. And yet Sister María Inés could still not decide whether the woman was motivated by deep faith or personal ambition, which was wholly inappropriate for a servant of God.

Sister Ana said curtly: 'My only desire is to fulfil my duties as best as my body and mind allow, Sister Teresa. I don't shirk from my obligations.'

'No you don't,' the other woman said. 'But sometimes one should take time off work to consider whether what one is doing is really what God expects or not.'

'This place is too small to allow us the privilege of ignoring each other,' Sister Beatriz said. 'We have to live together whether we like it or not.'

'That doesn't sound very noble,' Sister Ana said. 'But at least it is sincere.'

Sister Beatriz said: 'I think we ought to keep him. Whoever brought the baby here could've taken him to the orphanage or a church in the city. That can only mean they want us to keep him. We ought to respect their wish.'

'Whoever left him on the steps did not care for him,' Sister Ana said. 'You don't abandon a child you love.'

'Some people are simply too poor to look after a child,' Sister Teresa said.

'In that case,' Sister Ana said, 'they shouldn't have children.'

They had to wait for Sister Lucía to come back from the city to learn more about the baby. A little after seven they heard the Ford, and hurried to help the young novice with the provisions before it was time for the night prayer. It was dark when they assembled in the chapel, each holding a hurricane lamp. Although they were used to the Mother Superior's furtive ways, they did not notice that she was already there kneeling in prayer. Only when they blew out their lamps, sat on the pews and their eyes grew used to the dark did they see her taking shape out of the shadows and coming to the altar, the only sound that of her habit brushing against the floor. She began: '*Aperi, Domine, os meum ad benedicendum nomen sanctum tuum.*' Unlike noontime, she now led the prayers with great concentration, speaking with a moving voice while keeping her eyes shut throughout the service, shrouded in shadow except for her face, which, white and solemn, reflected the candlelight from the brass holders at either end of the altar. When the prayers ended, Sister Ana stood up to speak, but Sister María Inés raised her hand and stopped her before she had the chance to say a single word: 'Not here.'

The nuns lit their lamps and followed her across the courtyard to the refectory, where Sister María Inés asked them to sit. When she finally spoke, there was no hesitation in her voice. She said: 'The arrival of the child is nothing less than a miracle.'

The nuns had never heard her speak with such conviction. They all understood the significance of the meeting for what it was: a momentous occasion. The Mother Superior had the reputation of considering any decision for several days before making up her mind, and if that rule did not apply in this instance, it could only be because she was aware of something that they did not know themselves. But she had no intention of telling them what it was. 'Believe me,' she said. 'This is a matter between Our Lord and me.' Then she asked them not to doubt her piety or her good sense, but to accept the baby as a gift to the convent from God.

Sister Ana did not agree. 'Our life is one of prayer and renunciation, Mother,' she said. 'When we became nuns, we agreed to renounce all ties that bind us to this world, and that includes having children.'

'That child was not borne by one of us,' Sister María Inés said, pacing the room. 'And yet if we choose to keep him, then we choose to love him with a love that is even purer than the maternal love we have renounced.'

'That is deception not theology,' the other nun said. 'The result is the same: we have a child in our midst.'

'I say let's keep him,' Sister Teresa said. 'It'd be a blessing. All we do here is grow vegetables and flowers.'

'I agree,' Sister Beatriz said. 'I don't see how looking after a child could be incompatible with our mission.'

Sister Ana said: 'I understand the child is a boy. This is one more reason not to keep him. This is a retreat for women. It would be a sacrilege to have a male child living here.'

Sister Carlota said: 'Just like Moses.'

'Yes,' Sister Lucía said. 'But in a suitcase not in a basket of bulrushes.'

'He isn't ours, and he isn't Moses,' Sister Ana said. 'Who will take care of him? There are only six of us and our work takes up all our day.'

'There will be no changes to your daily schedule,' Sister María Inés said. 'I will look after him myself.'

'I would like to help too,' Sister Beatriz said. 'The problem is that a baby needs a woman's milk.'

'Not necessarily,' Sister María Inés said. 'I helped babies in Africa without a drop of it. One can mix ordinary milk with other things to make something similar to human milk. But it has to be in exact proportions. Only that way will a baby be able to digest it.' They had gone past the start of the Great Silence. The Mother Superior stood at the head of the table and rested her hands against it. 'Well, I thank you,' she said. 'There is nothing more to be said. Let me think about it. You may retire. Sleep in peace.'

The truth was that she had decided to keep the baby long before discussing the matter with the nuns, but nevertheless was pleased that all but one had given her their support. When Sister Ana passed by her to leave the room, the Mother Superior touched her on the arm. She said: 'I understand your reservations, Ana. But I have no doubt it is Our Lord's wish.'

The other woman paused and then replied with a few words in Latin that made the Mother Superior shudder: '*Crux sancta sit mihi lux. Non draco sit mihi dux.*'

Sister Ana walked out of the room and followed the other nuns in the cloister to the dormitory. Sister María Inés watched her in the moonlight until her shadow had disappeared in the corridors of the convent. Then she returned to her room, where she made sure the baby sleeping quietly wrapped in a blanket was well. She removed her wooden pectoral cross, kissed it and placed it on her bedside table, then took off her veil and her habit and arranged them carefully on a chair. In her flowing white undergarment, she lay softly next to the baby.

She had not paid attention to her hair before, the way she did not care about her body besides keeping it clean, which she did in a washtub filled with cold water even in winter: she did not approve of the indulgence of hot baths. But when she lay in bed that night, she noticed how grey her hair was, and for the first time became conscious of her age. She thought: 'I am an old woman,' with as much surprise as if it had only happened the previous night while she slept. She brought her head closer to the baby, and smelled the odour of leather from the old suitcase on his skin. She would have to make a cradle. She closed her eyes and thanked God for bringing the baby to her. She knew that it meant He had forgiven her. During the night she left her bed to warm some milk and feed the baby, and later she rose to go to nocturns. After the prayer she returned to her room and slept peacefully until just before dawn. Then she opened her eyes, and the words that Sister Ana had said to her in Latin the previous evening came back to her, making her shudder again: 'May the Holy Cross be my light. Let not the dragon lead me.'

S ister María Inés had good reason to believe that the arrival of the child at the convent was the work of Divine Providence. When she was nineteen years old and her name was still Isabel, she had answered a discreet advertisement in the newspaper. A few days after receiving a reply she took the train to another town in search of an address that turned out to be difficult to find. The three-storey art-nouveau villa with the gabled roof was far from the centre of the town, at the end of an interminable boulevard with palm trees on each side. Although Isabel had come on the agreed day, the shutters on the several bow windows were closed and there was no sign of life. Isabel rang the bell and waited long enough to think again about her decision before an unfriendly voice behind the door asked her name and rescued her from her mounting doubts. An old woman in a black dress allowed her to enter without a greeting and showed her into the parlour. Although the shutters on the windows facing the street were shut, an open door that gave onto an enclosed courtyard let in sufficient light.

The room had a tiled floor and was decorated with expensive furniture that smelled of beeswax. The potted tropical plants in the corners had grown out of control and threatened to swallow the paintings on the walls, but they kept the air agreeably cool in such an infernal summer. The woman who had let Isabel in studied her briefly with intense eyes and left without a word. The silence made Isabel tremble. In the years to come, she would grow accustomed to solitude and even reach the point where she would favour it over the company of people, but at that young age she still thought of it as a foretaste of the eternity of death.

Waiting for someone to come, she walked out to the courtyard, where birds hidden in a mass of dense ivy raised her spirits with their deafening noise. A piano began in an upstairs room and silenced the birds. Isabel sat on a bench and listened. Some time later the music stopped, a door opened across the courtyard and a tall woman in a black crêpe de Chine dress came towards her.

'Who are you?' the woman asked.

Isabel stood up. 'I've come for the piano lessons, madam.'

'Is that so?'

Round her neck the woman wore a gold chain ending with a pair of pince-nez, which she now raised to her eyes and studied her visitor. Isabel said: 'We have an appointment.'

'We do?' the woman asked. 'I have never seen you before in my life.'

'I . . .'

'Speak up.'

'I wrote to you. You replied a week ago.'

'Show me the letter.'

Isabel searched her handbag. The woman held her glasses to her nose and read the letter in silence. 'That explains it,' she said at last. 'You are early. Your appointment isn't until the afternoon.'

'I apologise. I took an earlier train in case it was delayed.'

The woman tore the letter up and said: 'Do not talk to me about train schedules. I am not a stationmaster. There is a reason why I receive only by appointment.'

'I could come back later.'

'Stay. It so happens that I am free.' The woman walked into the parlour and beckoned Isabel to follow her. 'Do you like the piano?' she asked, inspecting the overgrown plants with satisfaction.

'Very much.'

'And do you want to *learn*?'

'Yes.'

The woman fixed her with a stare. 'Are you certain?'

Isabel nodded.

'Good,' the woman said. 'Have you done this before?' Isabel shook her head from side to side. 'I see. Never before. There is no need to be afraid, child. Come with me.'

She opened the door and came into a hall where the old woman who had showed Isabel in stood holding a rolling pin. She looked at Isabel with mistrust, leaving her in no doubt that she would use it on her if her mistress gave her the order. But the other woman only said: 'Thank you, Bienvenida. It is fine. I will call you when I need you.'

The old woman nodded respectfully and let them pass. They made their way to the upper floor by a grand wooden staircase that creaked under their feet and entered a big room with a huge arched window. As soon as the woman closed the door, she became a different person. 'I am sorry, my dear,' she said and offered Isabel a seat. 'In my line of work we have to take precautions.'

'I understand, madam.'

'If only we did not live in the Middle Ages,' the woman sighed.

This room was also elegantly furnished with an upright piano, a heavy desk and a large ceramic fireplace. The walls were decorated with friezes painted with floral patterns that pleased the eye. The enormous window had no shutters, but its stained glass was enough to preserve the privacy of those inside from the prying stares directed up from the pavements of the boulevard. The room was cooled by an oscillating fan that rustled the papers on the desk with each pass. A door behind the desk was partly open, and Isabel saw that it led into a smaller room with medical equipment crammed round an operating table. The woman saw her staring at it, and went and closed the door. She said: 'Do not fear these things, my dear. They have been invented to help us. Do you really like music?'

'Was it you playing earlier, madam?'

The woman nodded. 'I am very fond of music. Also, it is good exercise for my hands. They are as important to a surgeon as to a concert pianist.' She patted her visitor on the shoulder. 'I apologise about the charade of the piano lessons. But I am told the Guardia have begun to suspect.'

'I know it is a serious offence.'

'Indeed it is.'

'Is there a chance we might get arrested?' Isabel asked, and looked at the door. She waited but nothing happened: all she could hear was the birds chirping in the courtyard.

'There is always the possibility,' the woman said. 'But don't worry too much. As you can tell by now, I take every precaution.' She sat at her desk and began to arrange her papers. She said: 'Believe me, I'm more worried about it than you. A prison cell would be much less comfortable than what I am used to.'

A horse-drawn cart went past outside, rattling the stained glass. Isabel held her breath until she could no longer hear it. She said: 'This is not the right time for me to have a child.'

The woman stopped her. 'I do not need to know, my dear. I am a doctor, not a cleric.' She finished clearing her desk and joined her visitor on the sofa. 'What I have to be certain about is whether it is your final decision,' she said, taking the girl's hand in hers. 'I hope no one has forced you to do it.'

Isabel shook her head and asked the question that had been tormenting her ever since she had received the reply to her letter: 'Is there danger?'

'I have several years of experience. There have never been any complications.'

'Will it hurt?'

'Only a little – afterwards. I'll give you some pills. Don't worry about that now. You'll be under ether.'

'I won't complain even if it hurts a lot. It was only fear that made me ask. Perhaps it *ought* to hurt.'

'Why, my dear, what on earth do you mean?'

'Since it's such a grave sin,' Isabel said. 'Don't you think, madam? I hope God will forgive me.'

'Like I said, I don't attend to the soul but only to the body. If you have any doubt, I suggest you go away and think more about it.'

The woman pulled a tasselled cord and her old assistant came. It was time. For several weeks Isabel had tried every herbal preparation, every poison, every patent medicine advertised in the newspapers to save herself from this moment but had failed. She followed the woman to the small room with weak steps and began to undress.

It all had begun with an afternoon walk to the Botanic Garden. The sun had been so strong that she had to seek refuge in the shade of the gazebo, where she sat with a book. It was a round gazebo with an iron railing, a domed roof and a single bench in the middle of an oriental arboretum with tall willows. She read for a long time with intense concentration, which was the way she always read (whether it was one of the latest novels or, years later, the religious manuscripts of the convent library), and stopped paying attention to the world round her. Her trance was broken when she heard footsteps: a young man in white uniform was coming down the path towards the gazebo. When he saw it was occupied, he hesitated for a moment, but then came and climbed the steps bravely, took off his cap and wiped his forehead on his cuff. Isabel shut her book and reached for her handbag.

'There is no need to go,' the man in uniform said. 'I am unarmed.'

'I was about to go.'

'No, you were not,' the man said. 'If my presence inconveniences you in any way, I should go instead.'

'You don't have to,' Isabel said quietly. 'There is enough room for both of us.'

The man bowed and sat down as far away from her as possible. He said: 'Thank you. I needed a little rest. It was very unwise of us to take a walk at this hour.'

They said nothing for a while. Isabel opened her book again, and the man fanned himself with his cap. Shafts of sunlight passed through the neat rows of trees in the arboretum. From where he sat, the man in uniform looked at Isabel and scrutinised the cover of her book. 'This is my favourite spot,' he said. 'I like to sit and listen to the leaves rustling in the breeze. Can you hear?' He was silent for a moment. 'Dead calm,' he said with disappointment. 'Not a puff of air today.'

And he fanned himself with his cap again. His immaculate uniform had gold buttons and a white leather belt from which a small ceremonial sword hung. Isabel noticed that despite the heat he wore his white gloves. He saw her looking at his hands and waited, hoping that she would speak, but time passed without Isabel giving any sign of doing so. Finally, he asked: 'And you, Miss? Do you come here often?'

She said that she did.

'You are very fortunate,' he said. 'Very fortunate. Where I come from, the nature isn't at all beautiful.'

This was his first year in the city. He was a cadet in the Naval Academy and came to the Botanic Garden as often as he could because it was the only place in the city to escape his classmates, who wanted to take him to taverns and places of ill repute. He said in dead earnest: 'But I refuse to be corrupted.' He took out his pocket watch and glanced at it, then stood up and put on his cap. 'Enjoy the rest of your day,' he said and left.

Later, when the heat eased, Isabel took a long walk, and saw him sitting alone at a table of the Garden café with a jug of water and a plate of sweetmeats. He bowed to her.

She saw him again a week later at a religious festival, among the crowd drawn to the revelry by the promise of miracles, and he saw her too, but before he had the chance to speak to her a group of nuns dressed in black carried him away in a torrent of ecstasy. The next time they met it was a Sunday and she was in the churchyard dressed in white with a wide muslin hat tied with a ribbon under her chin. He recognised her from a distance and approached her, amused by what she was doing: she had seeds in her pocket and was throwing them to a flock of parakeets that was jumping about her feet. He saluted and enquired whether she had been at the service.

'I come every Sunday,' she replied and continued to feed the birds.

'How strange we hadn't met till now.'

'It is a big church.'

'It's a big world too, but we still met.'

'In a church one should pay attention to the service not the congregation.'

'You talk like a priest.'

'You were standing on the left, near the pulpit,' Isabel said.

'So you did see me, after all.'

'Of course. One cannot fail to notice you.'

'You are flattering me.'

'I mean your uniform. It is impossible to miss in a crowd.'

They took a stroll round the churchyard. The service had long ended, and it was empty of people. Isabel asked: 'Do your studies allow you much time for recreation?'

'They let us out on Sundays and two evenings a week.'

'Is it enough?'

'Not since I met you.'

Isabel said nothing to that and they continued their stroll. She had finished school the year before, but had no plans to further her formal education. She liked to read, and once a week raided the bookshops for books on any subject as long as they were written in simple language. They talked a little more about what she had read recently, and then Isabel offered her hand. But the cadet did not kiss it: he took off his glove, and they parted with a handshake. His action made a good impression on her. They began to meet in the Botanic Garden on the two evenings a week the young cadet was allowed out of the Academy, and they took a long walk that always ended with him removing his glove and shaking her hand. Nothing more happened until one day, absorbed in conversation about the Age of Discovery, they lost their way in the Botanic Garden and came to an isolated spot where the path petered out into the overgrowth. Isabel said: 'I think we made a navigational error, Captain Columbus.'

She turned back, but he touched her arm. 'Yes, My Lady,' he said. 'But we discovered a new world that in my opinion is worth conquering.' He took off his cap and kissed her. Then, pleased not to have met any resistance, he said: 'Thank you. I come in peace.'

'I am not an Indian to believe you, Captain.'

'My proper title is Admiral of the Ocean Sea. And I have the honour of proposing a voyage.'

'Which you want me to fund?'

The cadet had had enough of the jest about the discovery of America. He looked at Isabel and said without smiling: 'I mean it. Let's go away for a few days.'

It was more than a month later that Isabel managed to find an excuse for their short holiday. They still took great precautions. Even though they travelled in the same train, they sat in separate compartments and did not speak to each other until they arrived at the seaside town that was their destination, a resort with old crumbling buildings. The town did not come alive until noon, and then it was as if one had stepped back into the beginning of the nineteenth century. Very old men and women in summer clothes came out of their hotels and pensions to take a stroll in the sun, ride horse carriages or sit in the cafés on the promenade. Then, early in the evening, while the sun was still very high, an imperceptible drop in temperature drove them all back to their hotel rooms, and they were not seen again until the following noon.

In those afternoons Isabel and the young cadet sat in their room, where he opened a large map on his knees and described to her his training voyages round the world. On their first day, he told her how the previous year his ship had been in Sicily when the big earthquake had hit, and the cadets had been sent to help recover the bodies buried under the rubble. When he finished telling the horrific story, he put away the map, undid his braces and began to remove his clothes. Isabel stopped him and continued to stop him the next two days. But on the last day of their holiday, she kept her composure, and while he undressed she also undressed with a steady hand. They lay naked next to each other in bed for a long time with the fan turning slowly on the ceiling, the carriages passing under the balcony, the curtains flapping across the open windows. When he lay on top of her, she pushed him off because all sorts of horrors crossed her mind. But it was only the momentary lapse of courage of a good soldier before his first battle, and she said: 'We have to be careful.' Then she overcame her fear and they made love for the first and only time in their lives, slowly, guided by instinct, with their eyes open, until the blood of her innocence soaked the starched sheets, passed through the mattress and a few precious drops fell on the floor.

When she had come home from her visit to the woman who was advertising her services in the newspaper, Isabel had had a long bath to rid herself of the smell of antiseptic and then slept for two days without interruption because of the ether. To her mother she said that she was running a fever. She slept without dreams and without pain, breathing quietly, lying on her back, her eyes fixed on the ceiling, her hands clasped over the covers like a reclining sepulchral statue. She slept so deeply that when she woke up she believed that she had never visited the woman and never had the operation. She kept the truth from herself until the effect of the ether passed off and the pain put an end to her intentional fantasy. She took two pills from the vial the woman had given her, but then remembered having argued that she ought to be suffering for her decision and regretted it. In church she had heard that the rigours of childbirth were God's punishment for the sin that Eve had committed in the Garden of Eden, and now thought that what she had done deserved even worse. So she threw away the pills to show her penitence, and the pain duly returned. For several days she could neither sleep nor leave her bed but only lie doubled-up under the blankets with her face buried in the pillow. Worst of all was the fact that she had to endure her suffering without a sound for fear that her parents would ask a doctor to examine her and he would find the truth.

She had asked the naval cadet not to write to her in case her parents intercepted his letter, but promised to let him know that she was well as soon as she could. A month passed and still she had not written to him. Once, from the window of her room, she saw him come to the house and stand at the door with his gloved hand stretched out for a long time, but then he turned back without ringing the bell. Finally, on a day of heavy rain, she simply put on her coat, took an umbrella and went to the Botanic Garden, knowing that she would find him sitting in the gazebo. He was there. She climbed the steps and sat on the other end of the bench, the way he had done the first time they had met. Each waited for the other to speak, but time passed with neither of them saying a word. Eventually the young man said: 'Please do something to show me you are alive.'

She knocked on the wood of the bench.

'Thank God,' the man said. 'I thought you were a ghost.'

'God has nothing to do with this.'

'Are you afraid?'

'I'm afraid of God.'

A wind out of nowhere carried the smell of jasmine. The man said: 'Do not be. God ought to be on the side of those who suffer.'

'Not the sinners,' Isabel said.

'The sinners need his help even more. It's they who suffer the most. He'll help us get over this.'

Isabel remembered their carefree past and said: 'I'm afraid of these uncharted seas, Captain Columbus.'

'There is no reason to be afraid, My Lady. Untold riches await us where we are heading.'

'I am not brave – and I cannot swim.'

'Our caravel is unsinkable. Nothing bad will happen to us again.'

And so they began to meet again on Sundays after church, no matter the weather, not only in the Botanic Garden but also other places where they would be safe from Isabel's parents and people who knew them. The day he was sailing for his last training voyage before being given his commission, Isabel went to the harbour to wave her handkerchief to him. He saw her among the crowd and waved back to her, but suddenly the wind snatched away the embroidered piece of cloth from her hand and it fell into the stinking waters of the harbour. Isabel ignored the bad omen and continued to wave her hand until the ship left port, the band stopped playing and the crowd began to disperse.

She never saw him again. Months later she learned from another cadet that he had died of typhus in the South Pacific and had been buried at sea. She had no doubt that God had punished him for their shared sin. She took to her bed and mourned him in total silence, without tears, without laments, without lighting candles. She knew that she was as much responsible for the misfortune as he had been, and thought it unfair that she was still alive while he lay on the bottom of the ocean on the other side of the world. Her worried parents, who had no idea about the affair, asked every doctor in the city to examine her. One after another they came to tap every part of her limp body with rubber hammers, brush the soles of her feet with goose feathers, listen to her heart with stethoscopes, shine lights in her eyes, and they concluded that she suffered from neurasthenia. They recommended the rest cure – that is, to stay in bed and avoid all human contact other than with the nurse who massaged, bathed and treated her with spoonfuls of tonics and a course of electrotherapy to revitalise her body with new energy. No one recognised the symptoms of grief until Isabel took the white dress she had worn the time she had met the young cadet outside the church, asked her maid to dye it black and began to wear it wherever she went. Over the course of time, she told her parents about the affair, but set their minds at rest by telling them that it had not been consummated. They forgave her, and in order to avoid any scandal also took to wearing mourning clothes, telling everybody they met that a relative who lived far away but whom they loved very dearly had passed on.

Isabel was convinced that not before long she would die too, but a year passed and she was still alive. One day she went to church and prayed to God with great devotion and honest desire to die there and then, but despite the tears and her repeated prostrations nothing happened. In the end she admitted defeat. 'Fine,' she said, wiping her tears. 'You don't want to do it now. I suppose You have Your reasons. But please, God, do it at Your earliest convenience.'

She was about to leave when a pigeon entered through a window and fluttered about in the church. A rain of soft down illuminated by the shafts of light fell over the pews, over the floor, over her black dress. It was then that Isabel had the inspiration, no doubt touched by the Holy Ghost, of becoming a nun to prove her penitence and to wait for the inevitable day when God would decide her punishment. More than thirty years later she was still waiting. And then, instead of the death that she was expecting, God sent Sister María Inés an orphan in a suitcase.

The reading that day was from *The Ascent of Mount Carmel* by Saint John of the Cross. Sister Teresa was sitting in a corner of the room reading in a clear voice while the other nuns ate with their eyes fixed on their plates. At the head of the table, Sister María Inés had eaten very little and sat in contemplation. The book was one of her favourites, and the moment Sister Teresa made a mistake, the Mother Superior shot her a stern glance.

'Please pay attention,' he said. 'You are not reading a comic paper.'

The nun corrected her mistake and continued. When all the nuns had finished their meal, they bowed their heads in silent prayer until the Mother Superior allowed them to leave the table with a single word: 'Amen.' They took their plates to the kitchen and served Sister Teresa, who was still smarting from the criticism. Sister María Inés did not notice; since the arrival of the child she thought of nothing but him. Indeed, before leaving the refectory she beckoned to Sister Carlota and told her: 'In an hour I will need some milk. Let it boil well and bring it to me while it is still hot.'

Sister Teresa looked up from her plate. 'When can we see the baby, Mother?'

'Not now – he is asleep. You can come later, when I will be feeding him.'

'He looks like an angel,' Sister Lucía said. 'I won't be surprised if one day he grows wings.'

The nuns cleared the table, washed the dishes and swept the floor. Then they were free until the afternoon prayer. After all these years Sister María Inés still did not understand why God kept her alive, but it was the companionship of those sisters and others who were now in heaven that had helped her preserve her sanity and deterred her from taking her own life.

The thought of suicide had first entered her mind the day she had heard about the naval cadet's death. She had then interpreted it as the natural reaction to hearing the terrible news, but several months passed and the idea of ending her life continued to dominate her thoughts. It was more than a wish to punish herself or a youthful fascination with death. Rather, it was a yearning for peace that lasted until the end of her life, even though she knew that death, in all probability, would not be the end of her suffering. Her mind was briefly freed of these thoughts when her venerable parents had died a few years apart. She did not attend their funerals, claiming that the telegrams had arrived too late for her to make the long and difficult journey, when the truth was that, despite her love for them, she had never ceased to think of them as the last remnants of a life that she no longer cared to remember: Isabel was no more. Nevertheless, she mourned them in the convent, saying novenas for the repose of their souls, unable to avoid her feelings of envy, for she knew that their time in Purgatory, whatever their mortal shortcomings, would be a great deal shorter than hers. Eventually, she did travel home to see the executor of her parents' wills and signed away her considerable inheritance from both sides of the family to charity, the money from the sale of the house, the furniture, the phaeton – everything – and returned to the convent consoled by the thought that the family line would die with her.

These days the impulse to end her life was no longer part of her daily contemplations, but it still crossed her mind from time to time, especially during Easter. On those occasions she would lie in bed with the windows open, and the air smelling of pine would soothe her sorrow without convincing her of the splendour of life. She had read what Saint Thomas Aquinas and Saint Augustine had written against suicide, but she still believed that it ought not to be a sin if one died of remorse and humility. To her mind the Passion was nothing less than the longest, most agonising, most selfless suicide in history. And yet in all her daring theological ponderings and moral conundrums there was one thing she had never imagined: that God would give her another chance.

She knelt in front of the crucified Jesus, touched his feet and crossed herself. On her way out of the refectory, she was approached by Sister Beatriz.

'I would like to help with the baby,' she said.

'I do not think you should come near him for the time being.'

Sister Beatriz was dismayed. 'Why not, Mother?'

'You were unwell this morning.'

'I am fine now, Mother. I can assure you that there is nothing wrong with my health.'

'Nevertheless, I cannot take risks. Babies are vulnerable to infections. You will be able to help later on.'

Before leaving the refectory, the Mother Superior reminded Sister Carlota again: 'Do not forget the milk. In an hour.'

Outside a warm wind that blew from the east lifted the dust in the courtyard. Spinning columns of air lashed against the walls and the windows of the convent with a deafening noise. Sheltered under the arches of the cloister, the Mother Superior blinked several times and paused to stare at the bell tower obscured by the haze of dust. On a chimney a family of storks was standing in its nest, indifferent to the windstorm. She walked along the cloister, keeping close to the wall to avoid the dust, and climbed the stairs to her room quickly, her breathing becoming heavier with every step. She used to pride herself on her physical strength, which allowed her to sleep only three hours a day and still be able to accomplish more than the other sisters, even those much younger than her, but her advantage had begun to disappear when she had turned fifty. When she reached the top of the stairs, she paused to push back her veil and wipe the beads of sweat from her forehead.

The baby had woken up. She took him in her arms, held him up next to the photograph of the young cadet on the wall and studied the two faces. All these years the naval cadet had been at her side, as young as she remembered him, dressed in his white uniform, the peaked cap, the gold-tasselled epaulettes, the ceremonial sword. They slept together, went to prayer together, worked side by side, ate in the refectory without the nuns having the faintest idea. She talked to him about anything, from the affairs of the convent to her eternal complaint of having grown old and tired of waiting for God to grant her wish to join her beloved in Purgatory, taking care to speak in a low voice and only when they were alone: otherwise, the nuns would think that she had lost her mind.

Some time later Sister Carlota brought the milk. The other nuns had come along to see the baby too. Sister Ana was among them. The Mother Superior asked the elderly nun to leave the milk on the desk, and handed her the child. While Sister María Inés prepared the food, the nuns crowded round Sister Carlota.

'Remember what I told you about your illness, Beatriz,' the Mother Superior said. 'Stand a little further back.'

The young nun obeyed.

'Does he cry?' Sister Teresa asked.

'Never. I try to keep him comfortable, but this bed is not

where a baby should be sleeping. Teresa, I need you to help make a cradle for him. We will need a few floorboards from the old school. Sister Ana will help you. Take them to the workshop where I will do the rest.'

Sister Ana said: 'I prefer not to be involved. I am very busy with my painting of the Transfiguration.'

'I'd be glad to help, Mother,' Sister Beatriz cut in.

While feeding the baby, Sister María Inés spoke to the two nuns who were going to help her. 'Be very careful with the splinters. The nails will be rusty so there is the danger of tetanus. Put on thick gloves and choose boards that are not warped and have no knots, otherwise it will be very difficult to cut and plane them.'

Sister Ana said: 'You are wasting your time. The machines in the workshop most likely don't work. They belonged to Saint Joseph.'

'I may have never done any carpentry, but I have enough experience with the Ford,' Sister María Inés said. 'I have no doubt that I can manage.'

After the baby had fallen asleep, she left Sister Lucía to watch it and went to the workshop. The door was stuck but she managed to open it with the tyre iron. Thick cobwebs hung down from the ceiling and the air smelled of wood and damp. She opened the windows and examined the machine tools: all they needed was fresh lubricant. She put on her smock and replaced the oil, then pulled down the cobwebs, washed the windows and swept the floor. The steam engine that powered the machine tools was outside the small building. It was very old and had steel wheels and a tall funnel like a train engine. Sister María Inés filled it with wood and lit the fire. The water had not yet boiled when the two nuns arrived with the floorboards. She stayed in the workshop for the rest of the day, breaking off only to attend prayers and briefly visit the baby. She stopped work sometime before the last prayer of the day and returned to her room to have a bath. Then she washed the baby too, with soap and a very soft brush, and wrapped him in several layers of clean cloth to carry him to the chapel. When the nuns came to prayer, she was standing at the altar with the child in her arms. She waved them to their pews and said: 'We ought to give praise to Our Lord for the miracle of this child.'

Sister Ana did not sit down but stood alone in the aisle with her arms by her sides and her fists clenched. She said: 'This is wrong.'

'If you do not agree, you are allowed to pray in your room,' the Mother Superior said.

'You are committing a sin. You know nothing about that child.'

'What I know is between God and me.'

'Nonsense,' Sister Ana said. 'You have lost your reason.' She turned to the other sisters. 'I suggest you all come with me before you commit a great sin.'

The women looked at her with confusion but made no move. Sister Ana knelt in the aisle, crossed herself and left the chapel, the yellow candlelight lighting her way. She was in the middle of the courtyard when she realised that she had forgotten her lamp and felt afraid of the falling dark. But she was too proud to turn back. She hurried to her room, muttering to herself, while back in the chapel the litany began.

S ister Ana walked along the cloister contemplating the statues of saints in the niches of the wall. She was alone and heard no sound other than her shoes on the flagged corridor but still looked over her shoulder from time to time. Beyond the colonnade was the courtyard and across the courtyard was the chapel. Its presence offered her a hint of strength. She had little doubt that the recent events were the work of the Devil. The clock on the bell tower said a few minutes past ten in the morning. At this time she should have been busy with her duties but she had asked to be excused from work, saying that she had slept badly. The Mother Superior had consented, but with a stony glare that made it clear she had not forgiven the nun's outburst in the chapel. Sister Ana did not regret what she had said the evening before: she had done her duty. She sat on a bench in the shade of the cloister and thought how she would defeat the Devil.

She had come to the convent of Our Lady of Mercy with the simple purpose of serving God as best she could, but had not escaped the ill fortune that had pursued her from childhood and condemned her to loneliness. By now she was beginning to think that perhaps she should not feel sorry for herself, for the life that she led could simply be what God had decided for her: His truest servants were always the hermits. She had nothing but scorn for the other sisters, who did not understand her. She believed that their light-heartedness was inappropriate. She thought of them as lazy and even doubted their devotion to God.

She took the rosary in her hands and began the Apostles' Creed: '*Credo in Deum patrem omnipotentem, creatorem caeli et terrae . . .'* Her fingers moved along the beads while she prayed in a low voice. On the bell tower a stork flew off with slow flaps of its wings and circled the convent a few times before heading away. Sister Ana felt pity for the world suffering from poverty and sin. She had great plans for the convent if only she were in charge. She wanted to turn it into a refuge for women who had been ill-treated and those who regretted their sins. The land for miles round belonged to the convent, and she was convinced that if there were more sisters they could farm it and make a big profit rather than just earning enough to feed themselves. It was the Mother Superior who stopped her from doing these things. She finished praying the rosary and came from the cloister to the courtyard, where she stopped at the well to drink. Then she went for a walk round the abandoned buildings, daydreaming about making the convent the best in the country.

Only the Bishop she considered capable of understanding her, but she had very few opportunities to talk to him. The only time they were alone was in the confessional once a month when he came to the convent. He was the person whom she admired more than any other in the world, and she looked forward to his visits. After Mass he sat down to lunch with the women. In summer they carried the long refectory table into the garden and ate under an overgrown muscatel vine, still fecund enough, despite its age, to produce white grapes with a superb fragrance and a very sweet taste. When the Bishop had first suggested that they eat outside, the Mother Superior had been unsure. He had made light of her objections. He had said: 'I understand that the Holy Father himself is very fond of eating alfresco,' and she had relented. Standing at the head of the table, he would say grace, and then they would sit to eat the baked fish with vegetables from the garden prepared in his honour. The Bishop updated them on the news from the world, told them amusing stories, brought them confections made with almond paste and flavoured with rose-water, which he offered to the nuns at the end of their lunch, going several times round the table with the box. The Mother Superior always declined but the nuns welcomed them with delight. The Bishop did not eat sweets either, not out of the fear of indulgence that stopped Sister María Inés but because of his teeth. He often joked that one of these days he would excommunicate his dentist, for having failed to save him from the curse of caries despite stuffing his mouth with more gold than there was in the city of El Dorado. After lunch he followed the Mother Superior to her office, where they discussed the affairs of the convent in between sips of coffee with a drop of milk. Then he blessed the nuns and climbed into his car to drive back to the city.

Sister Ana never told anyone how sorry she was to see him leave. His kindness had prompted her once to speak to him about her ambitious plans. She had been the last nun to confession and afterwards waited for him. He came out of the confessional, put on his amaranthine biretta and smiled at her. Sister Ana bowed and kissed his ring. 'Your Excellency,' she said. 'There is a matter I have been thinking a lot about lately.'

The Bishop took a glance at his watch and spoke in a friendly way. 'We could discuss it at lunch?'

'I'd rather not speak in front of the sisters.'

'If it is something you forgot in your confession we'd better go back into the box.'

The nun shook her head. 'It is not related to my confession, Your Excellency. But it concerns me greatly.'

The Bishop took off his biretta, sat with her on a pew and arranged his cassock with a noble hand. Then Sister Ana spoke to him of her various schemes to improve the income of the convent and ended with a solemn remark: 'This place could become a beacon of hope again.'

The Bishop nodded. 'I see you have thought carefully about this.'

'You have no idea how many ideas I have, Your Excellency. If only I had the chance to implement them.'

'Quite,' the Bishop said and quoted Archimedes with amusement: *Give me a place to stand and I shall move the earth.* Stroking the cross on his chest, he regained his solemnity and observed the woman with inscrutable eyes. After a moment he added: 'I believe you have great abilities, Sister Ana. Perhaps they are not put into their best use right now.'

'A certain person does not think so.'

The Bishop understood. 'Do you have any grievance against the Mother Superior?'

'She has shown no interest in my suggestions. All she has done is place obstacles in my way.'

The Bishop ran his fingers over the biretta on his lap. 'There are certain practices one ought to make a habit of,' he said. 'When one walks by a confessional, it is right to cover one's ears to show respect for the sanctity of confession even when no one is inside. Similarly the nuns ought to respect their Mother Superior even if they have reservations about her abilities.' Sister Ana tried to speak but he stopped her with a gentle gesture. 'That does not mean one should never voice one's concerns. But this should be made through the proper channels.'

'The proper channels are too far away to know what goes on in this unimportant corner of the world, Your Excellency,' Sister Ana said. 'All my letters to the Superioress General have gone unanswered. I suspect they have been intercepted. Although I should not be making accusations when I have no proof. The truth is that Your Excellency is my only hope. You have first-hand knowledge of our convent and its people. I respect your judgement.'

The Bishop consulted his watch and said: 'I will think about it and get back to you, Sister. Bear in mind that these things take time. Various enquiries have to be made.'

'I am grateful, Your Excellency.'

'In the meantime, I expect you to carry out your duties as usual. Remember you have taken an oath of obedience.'

The nun bowed her head.

'I hope there is no personal animosity between the Mother Superior and you. That would be very regrettable. I have to tell you that I hold her in great regard.'

'I only wish to see us do better, Your Excellency. At this rate of decline our convent won't survive for another generation.'

'These are difficult times,' the Bishop agreed. 'We can't compete against the storm of progress. But sooner or later things will slow down and we'll catch up. Christianity has been through worse.'

He stood up and offered her his hand. The nun bowed and kissed his ring. He said: 'You had better go now. We are late for Mass. The sisters are waiting. Please let them know we'll be starting in a few minutes.' He walked her to the door of the chapel. 'There are other options, of course,' he said. 'I hear the post of sister visitatrix will fall vacant soon. The present incumbent is getting too old to travel. It seems to me that someone with your vim and vigour would be ideal for it.'

Sister Ana felt the joy of being given a position that was highly regarded not only within the Order but beyond. Then she would be able to fulfil her innovative plans without having to worry about Sister María Inés.

'Of course, it is not for me to decide,' the Bishop said. 'But the Superioress is a good friend and always asks for my opinion about everything that goes on in my diocese. The next time I am in the capital I could mention your name.'

Sister Ana squeezed her rosary. 'That would be a great honour, Your Excellency.'

'I could also ask her whether she has received your letters.'

'Do not bother the Dear Reverend Mother with that matter. It is nothing. The letters must have gone astray in the post.'

The Bishop said: 'That would be my guess too.'

'I can always write to her again.'

'The post of sister visitatrix involves a great amount of travel across the country.'

'Your Excellency need not worry about that. Our Lord has blessed me with a very strong constitution.'

'You understand that I am not promising anything. I'm only mentioning it as a possibility.'

'I would not presume to say that I deserve such an honour.'

'It is not that, Sister. There are many issues I have to consider. Sometimes a bishop has to act the diplomat.'

That had been the end of their discussion. The Bishop had visited the convent a few times since but had not mentioned anything to her. Sister Ana understood the delicacy of the matter and waited patiently, convinced that one of these days the letter would arrive from the capital with the news of her appointment.

Lost in contemplation, she found herself near the old school for novices and walked in to assess its condition. The building had two storeys with wooden floors and thick walls made of stone. Despite the fallen plaster, the beams riddled with wood-worm and mould, the broken windows, the school could be restored and reopen to novices. She was certain that she could find many girls to join the convent. She came out of the building and one of Sister Carlota's stray dogs came wagging its tail. She let it follow her in her walk.

She had been only a child when she had seen the Devil for the first time, in the guise of a tall man in a black tailcoat, a beard without moustache and a stovepipe hat. He was a street scribe sitting at a desk in a funfair where he sold prophecies for a small fee surrounded by a big crowd. She had asked her father for a coin and dropped it in the cup on the desk. The man looked at her, then looked at her father, took a sheet of paper from his neat pile and dipped his pen in an inkwell filled with a thick substance that could only be blood. After he wrote something in crimson letters he took an envelope from under his hat, put the paper inside, sealed the envelope carefully and handed it to her with his long ink-stained fingers and a grin that was missing three teeth. Later, at home, she opened the letter and unfolded the paper, where it was simply written: *One year, six months and eleven days.* The words meant nothing to her then, but the following year, on the day foretold, her father dropped dead at the dinner table.

Sister Ana walked on, deep in thought. No one had seen anyone bring the baby to the convent or heard a mule or car. The nearest houses were more than twenty miles away, and nobody could have walked that distance with a baby in a suitcase. The sensible thing would have been to leave him somewhere in the city for the authorities to find. Sister Ana agreed with the Mother Superior that whoever brought the child to the convent wanted to offer him to them alone. The difference was that she did not believe it was God who had given him to them. The dog began to bark. She looked up and saw that it was digging close to the wall that ran round the edge of the convent. It dug out the corner of a piece of cloth and began tugging at it with its teeth. Sister Ana pushed the dog aside, dug up the rest of the cloth herself and saw with surprise and terror that the white piece of cloth was stained with blood that had long dried.

When the storks had first come to the convent, during the previous century, the nuns had thought of them as a good omen and a sign of future prosperity. The first pair had made its home on the top of the bell tower and in the following days more had arrived and built their nests on the chimneys. In those days they stayed at the convent only until late summer, and then flew to Africa, from where they returned again in early spring, their feathers covered in the yellow sand of the Sahara. But over the years they had discovered the rubbish tips round the city; and these days had no reason to leave until the weather turned cold in autumn. Then the nuns pulled down the empty nests to unblock the chimneys and lit the fires, but the following year the storks built them again as big and strong as the year before. Now that the nuns had abandoned many of the buildings, there was no need to destroy the nests, to which the storks added each year, until some were as big as boats. The nuns only stopped the birds from nesting on the guesthouse, where the chimney was always kept clean in case the Bishop wanted to stay the night when he visited the convent and asked them to light a fire. Every October, on the feast day of Saint Francis, they held a blessing in the courtyard for the storks and also the dogs that Sister Carlota brought to the convent. One year, a long time ago, a nun had climbed a ladder to look at the nestlings, but the big stork guarding them had stood up and flapped its wings, and the woman panicked and fell from a great height, dying on the spot. Sister María Inés was a young nun when it had happened. She never forgot the incident and when she became mother superior, she strictly forbade the sisters from going near the birds.

Today Sister María Inés had woken up earlier than usual to collect wood for the steam engine before going to dawn prayer. She put on her habit in the dark, fed the child so that he would not wake up hungry while she was out, put on her boots and lit her way to the woods with her hurricane lamp. She walked among the pine trees in search of firewood, shivering with cold in her thin habit. A few steps ahead, animals hidden in the undergrowth scurried away as they heard her approach. The dew had not yet evaporated and the hem of her habit became sodden, but she was too immersed in her task to notice. She collected as much wood as she could lift and carried it back to the carpentry workshop. She returned to the woods for more and kept going back and forth until it was time for the dawn prayer.

After prayer she resumed her task until she decided that she had enough firewood. She put on her smock, fired the steam engine and worked for a long time before she took a break. With her smock covered in sawdust, she stood at the door of the workshop and watched the storks. Sister Lucía came with a jug of water. Sister María Inés asked: 'Who is with the child?'

'Teresa. She asked Sister Carlota to let her have him for a while.'

Sister María Inés drank a glass of water and asked about the mood in the convent that day. All was well. Sister Ana was working.

'I hope she will be cured of her foolishness soon,' the Mother Superior said.

The steam from the funnel of the old engine billowed out over the roofs of the convent before it dissolved. The novice observed the strange machine with fear. She said: 'Sister Beatriz would like to start driving to the city again.'

'Good,' the Mother Superior said. 'It would be better if the two of you took turns so that you have some extra time for studying. You need to study more if you want to take your permanent vows soon, Lucía. Then it might be a good idea to do some missionary work.'

Africa and the mission hospital where she had served in her youth were Sister María Inés's fondest memories. She had arrived on the coast of Guinea without any idea of what to expect after an eventful voyage during which the ship ran aground and they were almost shipwrecked off the Canary Islands. It took her several days to recover her strength and travel inland to the mission station, which turned out to be a small village of mud huts hidden behind a haze of insects on the banks of the Benito River. Three years there would teach Sister María Inés the fortitude that stayed with her for the rest of her life. When she saw the endless caravans of patients who had travelled many days and hundreds of miles to get to the hospital of the White Fathers, she instantly knew that she could not have found a better place to atone for her sin. The moaning sick, the crocodiles floating in the muddy river, the humid air, the infectious laughter of the children, the calls of the turacos hidden in the treetops, they all merged into a hallucination which one did not escape even in sleep. It was the turn of the twentieth century, when diseases were treated with simple but effective medicines: leprosy with chaulmoogra oil, dysentery with syrup of ipecac, festering sores with mercuric chloride, malaria with quinine. Thanks to these and many other medicines, Africa ceased to be the white man's grave and colonists began to flood in. Very occasionally some good was done by the foreigners. In French Equatorial Africa, Sister María Inés had met Albert Schweitzer before the rest of the world knew him, and although she considered his Lutheran theology wrong she could not but admire his work.

She told Sister Lucía: 'The cradle will be ready tomorrow.' Then she noticed that something troubled the young nun. 'What is it, Lucía?'

'Do you intend to talk to the Bishop about the child, Mother?'

'Not yet. I have to think this over carefully. But I have no doubt that sooner or later we will need His Excellency. He has influence over the authorities.'

In reality she was not at all confident that he would help them. She considered him a man of sound judgement, but feared she would not be able to convince him that the coming of the child was a miracle unless she told him about the sin she had committed in her youth. Then he, too, would surely see that a miracle was the most likely explanation. But he would not forgive her: admitting such a mortal sin after so many years of not having confessed it warranted her dismissal from the Order. Her only hope was the tolerance for which the Bishop was known across his diocese, although it sometimes went beyond that of an enlightened cleric and came close to heresy. Once at lunch in the garden he had told the nuns: 'It's about time we canonised that old fellow Darwin.'

'There are some things I will need when you go to the city tomorrow,' Sister María Inés told the novice. 'Buy a few tins of white paint and a brush for the cradle; also this medicine to put into the child's milk.'

She gave her a piece of paper, and the novice read the list.

'What should I tell the pharmacist?'

Sister María Inés gave her a stern look. 'Only the truth – that is, I asked for them. Nothing more.'

The nun put the paper in her pocket. On the chimney of one of the abandoned buildings a pair of storks stood in their nest. The Mother Superior watched them with her hands in the pockets of her smock, while the steam engine shook noisily, sending billows of steam up in the air. 'One more thing, Lucía,' she said. 'And I want you to be very careful about this because it might upset Sister Carlota. It is about the rats. The traps are not enough.

We need poison. Now with the child we cannot afford to be careless. Rodents are carriers of disease. Buy a large amount. But do not tell anyone about it and do not put it in the storeroom. Bring it to me straight from the car. I will keep it safe.' Then she added, without having to look at the clock on the bell tower: 'It will be time to feed the child soon. I will walk back with you.'

The steam engine was cooling down, but out of prudence she opened the pressure valve and steam escaped with a hissing sound. She explained: 'Just to make sure the boiler does not explode.' She took off her smock and closed the door of the workshop with the intention of resuming her work after lunch.

They walked across the orchard, where the apples were almost ripe. The Mother Superior examined a few with her fingers without cutting them from the trees. She said: 'Our Lord offered me a gift I do not deserve. It is as amazing as if a broken branch of a tree had borne fruit.'

'You mean the child,' Sister Lucía said.

'A miracle is the only explanation. My window has a clear view of the road and you know how I like to stare out. I would have seen anyone coming from a long way off. But I saw nothing. Miracles are very rare in our time, Lucía. But this does not mean that they no longer happen. And when they do, the evidence is undeniable. The Miracle of the Sun was witnessed by a hundred thousand people.'

People still talked about what had happened some years before in Portugal, after three shepherd children had claimed that a miracle would take place at high noon outside the town of Fátima. When the day came, a heavy rain fell which drenched to the skin the people who had gathered, but then the clouds parted and a dull revolving sun cast the colours of the rainbow across the landscape. A moment later the sun began to drop towards the earth so clearly that many of those present believed it was the end of the world. It lasted ten minutes, during which the three children who had foretold the miracle also claimed that they could see visions of Jesus and the Virgin blessing the crowd.

'Miracles are specific to place and people, Lucía,' the Mother Superior said. 'In the case of the Miracle of the Sun it was seen only by people in Fátima and the surrounding areas. As one would expect, astronomers saw nothing. The laws of nature are suspended only for those humble enough to believe that God has unlimited power.'

A swarm of bees came towards them. Sister Lucía took a step back.

'Do not be afraid,' the Mother Superior said and walked on. 'They never sting nuns, because they cannot stand the smell of incense.'

The young novice followed her cautiously. She said: 'I always pray that you will live for many years to come, Reverend Mother. And when you leave us that you will be declared a saint.'

'That is an ambition I am not allowed,' Sister María Inés said, and bent down to cut some flowers. 'But what has happened makes me hope that perhaps I could make it as far as Purgatory.' She stood up with effort, gave the flowers to the girl and they walked along the cloister towards her room.

Sister Teresa wanted to see the child again. She knocked at the door and entered the room, where Sister Carlota was pacing up and down with the child in her arms. 'Let me have him for a while?' Sister Teresa said. 'I promise to be careful.'

Sister Carlota gave her a worried look. For a long time she had been trying without success to put the child to sleep, and although he was quiet she had to hold him because the Mother Superior had asked her to. She was behind with the baking of the altar breads and would have to work late in the kitchen that evening. She handed the other nun the child with a sigh of relief. 'Only a mesmerist could make him close his eyes,' she said. 'It is impossible.'

Sister Teresa began to rock the baby and sing to him. She had studied hymnody and sang in the chapel with a voice that had earned her the admiration of the other sisters, but her true love was popular music. She could imitate the voices of the famous flamenco singers of the time so well that the other sisters could not tell the difference. She could also sing Argentinian tangos, Cuban *sons*, Portuguese *fados*, even American jazz and English dance music, despite the fact that she did not know what the words that she sang meant. She borrowed the gramophone, which Sister Ana did not object to lending her, and played the records that Sister Beatriz secretly bought for her in the city. On Sundays, usually in the afternoon, when the other sisters were in the garden and the Mother Superior read in the library, she stole away to her room, wound up the gramophone and pushed a sock down its horn to reduce the volume. Then she sang along to the music, not too loudly but with great emotion, while keeping her eye on the door: if the Mother Superior knew, she would have punished her severely.

As she rocked the baby in her arms and sang quietly, the child looked at her with curious eyes. She sang about death, love and betrayal: a world of horrors. Her face, pale from the lack of sun and the strict diet, was not the face of a singer. Still rocking the baby in her arms, she gazed out of the window at the earthen road that twisted and turned through the pine trees and went out of sight down the hill. High in the sky, a few storks glided silently. She touched the baby's forehead with the tip of her fingers and paced the room, the wooden floor creaking under her feet.

She had never been alone in the Mother Superior's room before, and while singing she looked round her with curiosity. When she opened the wardrobe, the smell of mothballs made her sneeze. There were only a few dusty clothes and the boots that the Mother Superior wore when she went into the forest to collect wood. Then she saw the old suitcase in which the baby had been found and could not resist having a look inside. She pulled it out and, holding her breath, opened it, but the suitcase hid no secret, and she put it back. On the bed was a pile of bed sheets smelling of lavender: it was where the baby slept. Sister Teresa studied the portrait of the man in uniform about whom the sisters knew nothing. The baby opened his mouth and made a little sound. 'Sh,' the nun said. 'Let's see what other secrets besides you the world hides.'

She walked on, rocking the baby in her arms and humming a tune. She bent down and read the paperwork on the Mother Superior's desk, but it was nothing interesting: just bills and letters to women who wanted to join the convent. She opened a drawer and peeked inside: a stamp with a wooden handle, a few pencils, a penknife. Then, carelessly, she shut the drawer with a slam that scared the child. Immediately he began to cry. Sister Teresa gave him a terrified look. She said: 'Stop, little angel. You will land us in trouble.'

The child continued to cry. 'Please hush. Hush now,' she said and began to sing. The baby did not stop. 'Oh Mother of God,' the nun said.

She looked at the door with hope, but Sister Carlota was not coming. 'Oh, be a good boy and stop crying. Or we will both fall from grace.'

She walked up and down the room, with the baby in her arms. 'Sh. Oh, why now? You were such an angel . . .'

The baby was still crying and his face was turning red. There were tears in his eyes, and she wiped them on the cuff of her habit, saying, 'There, there.' She rocked the baby faster, looking at the door. She considered whether she should go to get Sister Carlota. She could not take the child with her: the Mother Superior might hear the crying. She was rocking him so nervously that all of a sudden she felt him slipping off her. She caught him – but he had been scared again and was now crying louder. 'Oh, hush, please,' she said. 'Why are you crying, sweet thing?' She rocked him, repeating, 'Oh, oh, oh.'

She walked to the windows and pointed out. 'Oh, oh, oh. Look at the little birds.'

She sang to him again, raising her voice above the cries, so that when the door opened behind her she did not hear it. A voice said: 'What is happening here?' She gave a start and quickly turned round. The Mother Superior was staring at her. Sister Lucía was with her.

'I don't know why he's crying,' Sister Teresa said and handed the baby over. 'He was so quiet a moment ago.'

Sister María Inés pushed back the cloth that covered the baby's head and searched it for bruises. She said: 'Tell the truth.'

'I promise. I did nothing to him.'

Sister María Inés continued to examine the child until she was convinced that he was not hurt. She covered his head again and asked: 'Where is Carlota?'

She received no answer. Holding the baby in her arms, she guided Sister Lucía through the preparation of his food. As soon as she began to feed him, the baby stopped crying. The door opened and Sister Carlota entered the room in a hurry. The Mother Superior gave her an angry look. 'I will decide the punishment of you two later,' she said. 'Now go away, all of you.'

The three nuns trooped out of the room and Sister María Inés sat on the bed holding the baby. He went to sleep in her arms while she continued to suffer from the terrible thought that he could have been harmed, and a feeling of mistrust stirred in her heart. She could not trust the nuns to do what she told them, to help her raise the child, who was her only hope of forgiveness in the world, and who had come at an age when she should have been thinking about wearing her shroud. She resolved to punish the sisters for their disobedience, vowed not to be lenient with anyone any more, decided never to allow Sister Ana to speak about the Devil and the child again.

She placed the sleeping baby on the bed and sat in a chair facing the window. She knew that there were people who hurt babies, even mothers and fathers who harmed their own children. In the mission hospital where she had worked, there had been cases of children with burns, cuts and broken limbs, and there had also been reported instances of infanticide: the newborn buried alive after the mother had died giving birth, a pair of twins killed because they were considered a bad omen, the little girl of a tribal chief sacrificed to bring rain. She knew, of course, that she was guilty of the greatest infamy too, for to her mind the end of her pregnancy years before amounted to nothing less than murder.

She was not surprised by Sister Ana's behaviour towards her. She knew that she was her implacable enemy ever since her last annual visit to the Superioress General in the capital. The elderly woman had held the post for half a century with a success that owed as much to her virtue as to her mastery of compromise. On her latest visit, Sister María Inés found her tired and complaining of her health.

'Life is losing patience with me, María Inés,' the old woman said.

'I am very sorry to hear you are unwell. What do the doctors say?'

'They no longer care. I am now under the jurisdiction of a funeral director.'

She invited the Mother Superior to sit next to her and listened attentively while Sister María Inés talked about the affairs of the convent. Then she asked something that she had wanted to ask her for a long time: 'Tell me, is there any problem with your nuns?'

Sister María Inés was taken aback at the question. 'I do not believe so, Mother General.'

The other woman walked with great effort to her desk, opened a drawer and took out a bundle of letters. She placed them on top of her desk and pointed at them with a mocking finger. 'These say that you are incompetent,' she said.

Sister María Inés looked at the letters from where she sat.

'I guess you know who they are from?' the Superioress continued. 'You should know that I have answered none of them. I do not approve of intrigue. Remind me again who Sister Ana is.' A few clues were enough for her to remember. 'Oh yes. She has caused trouble before, hasn't she?'

'She came to us from the convent of the Heart of Jesus,' Sister

María Inés said. 'She believed that she was being persecuted there.'

'I know the matter. What I had been told at the time was that she had an inordinate ambition.'

'She still does,' Sister María Inés said.

'The line between serving God and trying to take His place is rather thin. Do not take it to heart. She probably thinks that prayer is not enough. She wants to offer Our Lord practical help. She has great faith in her abilities.' The Superioress General sighed. 'An *innovator*, God help us – just like the builders of Babel.'

'As a matter of fact, she does speak several languages,' Sister María Inés said.

'Do you want me to write to her?'

'It might make things worse. She causes no real problems. I suppose her clerical skills *have* proved useful. Oh – and she showed us how to dig an artesian well.'

The Superioress General put the letters back in the drawer. 'An artesian well? As you wish. But in your place I would be careful.'

When Sister María Inés had returned to the convent, she had told Sister Ana nothing about her conversation with the Superioress General, but had begun to watch her more closely, unsure what the nun might try next, yet certain that she would not cease to behave in a manner that took her further away from the path of God.

The child slept quietly on the bed. She took the rosary that hung from her belt and prayed for a long time until she realised that she had missed lunch. She was still angry at the two nuns who had disobeyed her instructions about the child. She did not want to eat and did not want to see anyone right now, not even at the refectory table, where they did not speak to each other. She begged the Virgin's pardon for having interrupted her prayer and resumed with closed eyes, every Ave Maria and Gloria Patri taking her a step closer to Heaven and giving her strength. But despite her effort to concentrate she soon strayed again from her contemplation and began to think about Sister Ana and how she, Sister María Inés, ought to put an end to her mutiny once and for all.

The discovery of the bloodied cloth convinced Sister Ana that the convent was visited by evil. Terrified but determined to thwart the plans of the Devil, she told no one what she had discovered. She did not know whom she could trust. There was always the possibility that not just the Mother Superior but also some of the other sisters were possessed. She spread the cloth out on the floor and examined it. She had assumed that it was a shroud but now saw that it was really an ordinary bed sheet. There was no doubt that it was stained with blood. She traced the stain with her finger, suspecting that it had to do with a ritual animal sacrifice. She crossed herself, repeating: 'Almighty God, father of Our Lord Jesus Christ . . .'

Her room was on the upper floor of the dormitory, at the far end of the loggia that overlooked the courtyard, past several rooms where no one lived any more. She had chosen that room herself, seeking peace and quiet in a place that could not be more peaceful. On an easel by the window stood a small painting of the Transfiguration with an unfinished Jesus floating in the air above the figures of Saints Peter, James and John. On a table next to the easel was a palette, together with many brushes and knives for impasto all cleaned and arranged in size. Sister Ana had taken up painting only a few months before but was already on her second painting. She hoped to finish this one and two more by the end of the year, all with themes taken from the life of Jesus, and present the Bishop with the best painting. She folded the bloodied cloth and hid it under her mattress, then thought better of it and put it in a box and the box in a drawer. She felt her confidence return: she had God on her side.

Over the next few days she searched every corner of the convent for other evidence of demonic rituals, taking care not to give rise to suspicions. She did not miss any prayer, carried out her daily duties with the eagerness the Mother Superior had come to expect from her and no longer protested about the baby. In her spare time, she took a spade and pretended to go to the garden, but as soon as she was out of sight she strode up to the wall that ran round the convent and began to dig near where she had found the bloodied sheet. She found nothing and decided to search the derelict buildings of the convent.

One afternoon she pushed the door and entered the school for novices. The air smelled of decay and was filled with dust that reflected the light like a curtain made of gauze. Clutching her rosary she searched the empty rooms, terrified less by the Devil than by the floorboards, which, damaged by rot and wood-worm, might give way at any moment. Most of the furniture had been carried off to be sold or used in other parts of the convent, and the only pieces that remained were those too damaged to be of any use. She came across nothing on the ground floor that aroused her suspicions. She lit her hurricane lamp and searched the cellar, but there was nothing there either. Then she took the stairs up to the scriptorium, the room with the big windows where in the old times the nuns used to copy manu-scripts to stock the convent library, and it was there that she finally found what she was searching for.

In a corner of the otherwise squalid room, under a pile of rolled parchments eaten by the rats, she noticed that the floor had been scrubbed clean very recently. Short of breath from having climbed the stairs, she knelt down and studied the floor-boards in the light from the big windows and her lamp. Along the joints, where the scrubbing brush had not reached, there were traces of blood. She shuddered at the thought that somewhere among the lecterns and parchments scattered about the room might still lurk the demon invoked by the evident ritual. She kissed the cross on her rosary and quickly made her way out of the building. The autumnal sunlight slanted over the roofs of the convent and through the arches of the cloister, where she went to sit. For a moment her mission felt too great for her. She was only a nun in a distant corner of the world, and even though she believed she could achieve many things in life if she set her mind to them, she doubted whether she could fight the Devil all by herself. A voice close by greeted her. It was Sister Beatriz.

'Where did you come from?' Sister Ana asked.

'You left in a hurry after lunch.'

'I had to work on my painting. There is still a lot to do.'

'Are you still worried about the baby?'

'You know what I think,' Sister Ana said. 'Am I the only one who has not taken leave of her senses? The baby should be in the orphanage. Our vocation is the contemplative life. There are things appropriate to our calling that we should commit ourselves to.'

'An orphanage is not the best place for a child to grow up,' Sister Beatriz said.

The other woman shrugged. 'We live in isolation. Let's suppose the child falls ill one day.'

'The Mother is a trained nurse.'

Sister Ana waved her away but did not protest when the other woman sat next to her. They stared at the well in the courtyard, the chapel behind it, the bell tower with the stork nest. Sister Beatriz said cautiously: 'I saw you walking round the old buildings earlier.'

'I like to walk. It's good for my indigestion.'

'You spent a long time inside the old school. I thought it strange.'

'Many things seem strange lately. I have been saying so, but none of you want to listen.' Sister Ana glanced round. There was no one else in the cloister. She leaned over to the other nun and added: 'I have no doubt the Mother is possessed.'

The bell sounded the Ninth Hour. The two nuns joined the other sisters crossing the courtyard on their way to prayer. In the chapel they sat separately. Later that evening Sister Beatriz went to see Sister Ana in her room. She was standing at her easel working on the Transfiguration. She asked: 'Has anyone seen you coming?'

Sister Beatriz had come across no one. The other women were all in their rooms. Sister Ana continued to paint with her back to her for a while, and then she stood back and asked her her opinion about the painting. Sister Beatriz came closer. 'You have talent, Sister. You ought to paint something on the wall of the refectory.'

'You mean a fresco. The Mother thinks it would be an indulgence.'

She picked up another brush and returned to her work. She painted with great concentration and a steady hand, her nose almost touching the canvas. Sister Beatriz stood and watched while the evening grew darker and the owls in the roof began to coo. Finally Sister Ana put down her palette and cleaned her brushes with turpentine. 'Now,' she said. 'Let me show you.'

She took the bloodied sheet out of its hiding place and spread it out on the floor. 'Mother of God,' Sister Beatriz said and crossed herself.

'It was buried on the far side of the convent. I found it by chance.'

Sister Beatriz pointed a finger at the stain.

'Blood, of course,' the other woman said. 'It is unmistakable.'

'Do you think that someone had an accident?'

'Accident? You talk nonsense. Why would someone bury it? And so far out of the way?'

'Perhaps it had been there for many years.'

'It doesn't look old. The rain and the worms would have ruined it.' She knelt down and began to fold it up. 'Besides, it's not the only piece of evidence.' She put the sheet back in its box and told the other woman what she had seen in the scriptorium: 'The floor had almost no dust at all. It appears to have been cleaned recently. I have no doubt. Someone had scrubbed the blood well, but it had trickled into the gaps between the floorboards.'

Sister Beatriz shook her head. 'But why would someone do all that, Sister?'

'It must have been some ritual.'

'A ritual?'

'A sacrifice – some animal,' Sister Ana said and added in a lower voice: 'I believe it was one of Carlota's strays.'

'Do you think *she* is behind all this?'

'Who – Carlota? Oh no, poor Carlota is quite harmless. One never knows, of course . . . but I think it's very unlikely. I can't say the same for the Mother. Her behaviour has been very questionable lately.'

'Because she wants to keep the child? Do you think he has something to do with this?'

'Naturally. The coming of the child and the ritual seem to have happened at about the same time.'

'So you think the Mother brought him to the convent, Sister?'

'Perhaps. Don't ask me where she found him – I have no idea. And I don't know what she intends to do with him. Maybe she plans to use him in another ritual. Of course, there is an even worse hypothesis. Maybe she didn't bring the baby *herself.* Maybe she performed the ritual to ask for the baby.'

'Ask whom?'

'Satan, of course.'

'It's only a baby, Sister Ana.'

'He does seem human, yes. But Satan has great powers of deception.'

'You don't really believe that.'

'If you believe in God, you shouldn't doubt the existence of evil.'

Sister Beatriz said: 'I mean that cases of demonic visitation are very rare. And besides, I doubt the Devil would dare come into a convent. It's a place that is guarded by God.'

'Exactly,' Sister Ana said. 'It is what makes churches and convents even more desirable targets for him. Corrupting people like us is a greater victory than corrupting someone who is not devoted body and soul to God.'

'God help us,' Sister Beatriz sighed.

Sister Ana said: 'There may be more evidence around but I couldn't find it. In any case,' she added and tapped the box containing the bloodied cloth, 'this will be enough for the Bishop.'

'The Bishop?'

'The Bishop. I trust him to act. But I will need your help, Beatriz.'

'What can I do, Sister?'

'Have you started to drive again?'

'The Mother says to arrange it with Lucía.'

'Good. You will take me to the city, and the two of us will go see His Excellency.'

Sister Beatriz did not like the idea. She said: 'Perhaps we should make an appointment first.'

'We have no time to waste. Let's just hope he's in the city when we go.'

'But he's a very busy man. He might have no time to see us.'

'He will,' Sister Ana said. 'His Excellency is a very good friend of mine.'

Before they parted, and although it was very late, Sister Ana insisted that they knelt and prayed to God and the Virgin to grant them courage. Then she anointed the doorpost and the window frames with oil from her votive lamp and gave some to Sister Beatriz, urging her to do the same in her room to keep out the Devil.

After terce Sister Carlota and Sister Teresa came to see the Mother Superior and admitted that they had made a serious mistake by disobeying her instructions about the care of the baby. They stood in the middle of the room with bowed heads and spoke in low voices, occasionally raising a contrite face to peek at the Mother Superior from under their veils. Seated at her desk, she listened to them with an expression that gave no hope of clemency. She had decided that being lenient with Sister Ana had been a mistake and was prepared to mete out an exemplary punishment. She wanted to warn all the sisters that she would not tolerate a disobedience whose consequences might be graver than any of them suspected: it could deprive her of Purgatory. Sister Teresa denied that she had done anything to hurt the child; her only mistake was that she had not guessed he cried because he was hungry. She let out a torrent of apologies and honest regrets, which she repeated over and over again while Sister Carlota nodded in agreement. The Mother Superior raised her hand.

'Enough. Your regret is sincere. But the fact remains that you were in a place you were not supposed to be, doing something you were not asked to do.' She tapped her fingers on the desk, thinking. Then she asked: 'Was it you, Teresa, searching through my wardrobe?'

'I was looking for something to wrap the baby. I thought he was crying because he was cold.'

'Do not lie to me.'

'The fact of the matter is that the child suffered no harm,' Sister Carlota said.

'*Deo gratias*,' the Mother Superior said. 'I asked you here today to prevent anything bad from ever happening to him.'

Next to her bed in the cradle she had just finished making, the child lay wrapped in a blanket. Sister María Inés repeated in her mind that she would devote herself to him and God; she would become someone else, humbler and more repentant. At long last she could say that she ought not to be burdened with the sin of her youth any more – but it was not for her to decide.

She cleared her throat and faced the two nuns waiting in silence for her judgement. After she had threatened them with all-night vigils, extra daily tasks, the torment of thirst and even expulsion from the convent, threats which satisfied her anger, the Mother Superior ruled that they were not to join the other sisters in the refectory for recreation at the end of the day but go to their rooms and do solitary penance for two weeks. The two women bowed. The Mother Superior fixed Sister Teresa with a stare of further disapproval and added: 'Our convent is not an inn where you can sing popular songs whenever you are seized by the muse, but a place of work and contemplation. Everything we do, at any time of day or night, whether awake or asleep, should aim at exalting the glory of God.'

'Yes, Mother,' the woman said.

'If you have to sing, then sing a hymn or psalm of our faith. There are enough not to have to resort to the ravings of drunken gypsies.'

Having nothing more to say, she dismissed them with a gesture of disdain. When she was alone again, she occupied herself with her daily ritual of remembering her fiancé. She topped up the lamp that hung next to his portrait, changed the burned wick and lit it. Then she knelt and crossed herself with a devoutness that one who did not know her would suppose directed not at the memory of the naval cadet but at the saints in the icons on either side of him. All these years she had been tormented with the idea that she was responsible for his death because it was she who had suggested they put an end to her pregnancy. She had suggested it without assurance, shaking with fear, hoping that he would reply with the inspired answer that she had missed in her nights of sleepless deliberation, one that would get them out of the mess without the necessity of sin, but his gratitude when he heard her suggestion was enough to convince her to do it. She did not know what would have happened if she had never proposed it. Although in all probability he would have asked her to do it, she chose to believe that he would not have demanded it and, consequently, she now thought that her share of the blame was far greater than his. Yet he was the one who had paid for it with his life. It was an ingenious punishment, for in that way she suffered from guilt both for her decision and his death.

Before the arrival of the child, she used to believe that if she were ever to be forgiven it would only be in the hereafter, so long as she had served God with humility while she lived. No one could say she had not been sincere in her remorse. To make amends she had travelled as far as the equator, where something had happened that had given her the opportunity to put the past behind her and start a new life, but she had chosen not to do so.

She had been in Africa for some time when a new doctor arrived from Europe and the director of the mission hospital introduced them and asked her to show him round and help him settle in. Sister María Inés, who remembered her own confusion when she had first arrived, was pleased to be the new doctor's guide. His work in the hospital was invaluable even though he was an ordinary surgeon without any training in tropical medicine. Sister María Inés did everything she could for him, but she was only a nurse with a practical knowledge of medicine. His true training was done by shadowing the director of the medical mission and reading books and journals sent from abroad. Then *he* began to help the nun improve her skills, and thanks to her commitment she soon knew far more than was expected from her. Their collaboration was productive and exemplary until a mosquito from a mangrove swamp flew to the mission with the sole purpose of passing through a hole in the net over Sister María Inés's bed and biting her.

She caught malaria but refused to admit it, as if that was going to cure her. For several days she carried out her duties despite feeling unwell, until one morning she collapsed in the ward while giving a patient his medicine. She spent several weeks in bed suffering from fever, tremors and cold sweats before starting to get better. It was only during her convalescence that the doctor and she became good friends and began to discuss other matters besides medicine. Every evening after he finished work, he came by to take her temperature, listen to her lungs with his stethoscope, palpate her liver and spleen while she kept her arms crossed over her chest and her eyes firmly shut, and give her a quinine injection. When he finished examining her, he helped her put back on her nightdress with painstaking respect, told her that he was done and sat at the open window some distance from her bed to smoke. The nun remained deadly still and silent. He was amused by her embarrassment at having allowed herself to be seen naked, but he understood how she must have felt and did not press her to speak or acknowledge his presence in any other way. Instead he sat back and told her the news of the day in a calm voice, and when he finished his cigarette he picked up his bag, wished her goodnight and went out, leaving behind a cloud of smoke that did not dissolve for a long time afterwards.

Later Sister María Inés would say that malaria was the reason she returned home, but this was not the whole truth. One evening, when she was almost well again, she conquered her embarrassment and opened her eyes as soon as the doctor had finished examining her and was helping her with her nightdress. He pretended not to notice.

'Thank you, Doctor,' she said.

'There is no need,' he said, taking off his stethoscope. 'I have a vested interest in your speedy recovery, Sister. As long as you're bedridden, I have to do your work too.'

'I thank you anyway. Although perhaps it would have been better to let the disease take its course.'

The doctor laughed. 'What silly bravado! You know if I'd left you untreated you could've died.'

She knew it. She had seen it happen countless times, even with patients who had managed to make their way to the hospital. But while she was confined in bed she had the time to wonder what her torment of fever truly meant, and had decided that it was the longed-for punishment for her mortal sin. She had then tried to tell the doctor not to treat her but let God decide what to do with her. She had waved him away, knocked the syringe off his hand, wrapped herself tightly in the bed sheets, but did not have the strength to make herself understood. The doctor had interpreted her behaviour as the symptoms of delirium and rushed to reassure her that she was not going to die, even if her suffering felt like standing on the threshold of death. That evening, when she was finally out of danger and had regained some of her strength, she repeated to him her wish to die in a clear voice. The doctor finally believed her. 'Well, Sister,' he said, taken aback. 'Why would you want to die?'

'I have my reasons, Doctor.'

'Think of your work here. You do a lot of good, you know.'

'Oh, the hospital is important, yes. But I personally am not. Another sister would be as good – if not better.'

The doctor asked: 'Isn't it a sin? When one is wishing for one's own death?'

'Not if it is also God's wish.'

'God's wish? I would guess He doesn't want anyone dead.' The doctor scratched his head. 'But I wouldn't know . . . Perhaps we don't believe in the same god.'

The nun frowned. 'What god do you believe in, Doctor?'

'Hippocrates – the god who saved your life.'

'I forgive your lack of faith,' Sister María Inés said, 'as long as it doesn't turn into cynicism. And now I am ready to return to my duties.'

She got up from her bed and in her white nightdress, which covered her from the neck to her ankles, went to where her nun's habit hung. The doctor followed her with his eyes and said in a serious voice: 'Don't put it on.'

'Don't worry, Doctor. I feel perfectly well.'

'I know you do. But don't put it on all the same.'

The nun asked: 'Do you think there is still danger?'

'None at all. I was only wondering whether you really have to carry out your duties in those clothes.'

'My habit? Do you mean to say that I should stop serving God?'

'There are many other ways to serve Him.'

'Naturally – but I have chosen mine.'

'I don't think God would object if you chose a simple nurse's uniform.'

'Don't think you can understand His will for a moment, Doctor.'

The doctor took a step towards her. 'I'm talking of marriage,' he said.

'Well, it is not possible.'

'Why not? A marriage has the blessing of the Church, hasn't it?'

'Forget it. This habit means I am already married – to God.'

The doctor took her hand in his. 'Oh, divorce the old codger then.'

She freed her hand and slapped him across the face with as much strength as she had in her weak state. The doctor rubbed his cheek. 'Well,' he said. 'At least now we are sure that you are in good health. In fact, Sister, you're much better than I supposed. I guess I ought to have proposed to you while you were still delirious. You could hardly lift your hand then.'

'My lips would have given you the same answer.'

'Who knows?' the doctor said. 'Sometimes malaria impairs the brain.'

With a stubbornness that defeated his reassurances, she insisted that they could no longer be friends or even work together, for she could not look at him again knowing that when he was examining her he was thinking of other things than the health of her liver. And so, with a heavy heart, she decided to leave the mission, although he offered to go instead. A month later she was back in Europe, where she joined the convent of Our Lady of Mercy and gave herself over to her perpetual mourning, which only ended the day she held the orphan in her arms.

In the evenings, when she retired to her room, her mind always drifted to the past. As soon as she blew out the candle on her bedside table her room filled with the armies of demons she had read about in the medieval books kept in the library: demons of fate, goblins, incubi, familiar spirits which offered to serve her, shape-shifting spirits which crept into her room through the cracks in the door and tried to possess her. A couple of times a year, she still suffered from sudden shivering followed by high fever, and then sweating which finally brought down her temperature and left her feeling exhausted. It felt like malaria but she could not believe that she still suffered from a disease which she had caught so long ago. Instead she thought that it too must be another battle in the unending war between angels and demons over her tormented soul.

S ister Ana's theories upset Sister Beatriz. She left the other nun's room trembling from what she had heard about satanic ceremonies and blood sacrifices. She had listened with dismay before starting to say that she did not believe in all that, but Sister Ana had looked at her with suspicion and so Sister Beatriz had rushed to reassure her that she was on her side in her fight against the Mother Superior. She walked in the dark, keeping close to the wall and counting the doors along the loggia until she came to her room. She locked the door behind her and dropped onto her bed without taking off her habit. On the afternoon she had spotted Sister Ana searching in the courtyard, a sense of foreboding had driven her to follow the older nun from a distance across the grounds of the convent. Her intuition had proved correct. She had seen her pick up the bloodied cloth that the dog had dug out of the ground. She continued to shadow her and a few days later, holding her breath behind one of the pillars in the cloister, she saw Sister Ana walk into the derelict school for novices. She wanted to know what the other nun had discovered, but had been unprepared for the incredible theories that Sister Ana had just confided to her.

She stayed in bed all night, but did not manage to get a moment's sleep. She could not get what she had heard out of her mind. The silence turned every noise into a portent: the creaking of the floorboards, the windows rattled by the wind, the calls of the owls. A sinister thought made her shudder: perhaps Satan was truly in the convent and would not go away until he had destroyed them all; he had not been summoned by dark ceremonies, as Sister Ana imagined, but by the arrival of an innocent baby. She began to see how it could have happened. She always thought of the Mother Superior as a sensible woman and benevolent leader, but had struggled to explain her behaviour since the discovery of the newborn. The Mother Superior did not simply want to keep it, but had gone much further than that: she behaved as if the child were hers and doubted the loyalty of the nuns who, apart from Sister Ana, wished to help her.

When the bell rang in the middle of the night, Sister Beatriz lit her lamp and went to nocturns, where the Mother Superior led the prayer with the child in her arms. The same thing happened at dawn and again at prime, so Sister Beatriz decided to speak to her and try to make her see sense. She found the Mother Superior in her room, sitting at a window and soaking up the sun. After a night of having tried to carry out her religious duties and at the same time take care of the child, she was tired and melancholy. Sister María Inés made a vague gesture and the young nun approached and bowed. She said: 'I have come to offer you my help, Mother.'

The Mother Superior looked at her through her lethargy. 'Very kind of you,' she said. 'But everything is under control.'

The cradle was in a corner of the room. Sister Beatriz walked up to it and looked at the sleeping child. The Mother Superior shut her eyes and leaned her head against the window. When the young nun turned round and saw her, she said: 'Mother, you seem very tired.'

The Mother Superior opened her eyes again. 'I am fine.'

'Let me help you with the baby.'

'No. I can take care of him alone.'

The nun looked straight at her. The Mother Superior's white habit glowed in the sun but her black veil obscured her face like a shadow. Sister Beatriz said: 'But, Mother—'

'Be quiet. The child is asleep.'

They did not speak for a while. Suddenly the Mother Superior said: 'You might think that I have lost my mind, Beatriz . . . But I have thought carefully about this. The Blessed Virgin did not conceive Our Lord in the normal way. Yet she is still his mother, is she not? God entrusted His son to her. In the same way, I have assumed responsibility for this orphan – with great humility.' She crossed herself and added: 'The child's coming is an act of Divine Providence, Beatriz. I do not intend to explain to you why, for it is a matter between God and me. But do believe me when I say that I have no doubt about it whatsoever.'

Sister María Inés stopped and listened to the child breathing. He slept wrapped in a blanket while all round him hung the charms the nuns had placed to protect him from harm. But no charm could save her from her hallucinations when the icy winds that shook the pine trees on the hillside blew open the windows and announced the end of the world. In her brief sleep the previous night, Sister María Inés had had one of her familiar nightmares. She had heard, coming from far away, the howling of evil spirits, the laments of hermits who had given in to sin, the chants from a witches' sabbath where the servants of the Devil were dancing naked, trampling the Cross, eating the flesh of children and were being baptised in the name of Lucifer. Lying under her thin blanket and shaking from cold and fear, Sister María Inés had begun, with tears in her eyes, a long prayer to the Virgin and had not stopped until the light of dawn rescued her from her ordeal.

Sister Beatriz said: 'Reverend Mother, I have to talk to you about a very serious matter.'

It was no secret that the Mother Superior hoped the young nun would take charge of the convent after her retirement. They often went on long walks, just the two of them, and discussed not theology but practical matters that had to do with the running of the convent. Over the course of time, Sister María Inés had come to admire the young woman's common sense and unassuming manner, which did not show the slightest trace of conceit. She had never asked Sister Beatriz about her life before she had joined the convent of Our Lady of Mercy, where she was born or what her name was; she had only asked her to choose the name that she wished to be known by from then on. The young woman had shrugged and Sister María Inés had chosen one for her.

'You ought to be careful, Mother.'

'You are talking about Sister Ana.'

'She thinks you are possessed by Satan.'

'Ah yes, Satan. Do not mind her, Beatriz. What lies at the root of her attitude is not malice but her ambition. Perhaps I should suggest she move to another convent.'

The young nun sat down next to her wanting to speak but then lost her courage. The Mother Superior said: 'If you have something to say, say it.'

Sister Beatriz told the Mother Superior about Sister Ana's intention to ask the Bishop to intervene, but she did not tell her about the bloodied bed sheet or the evidence of strange goings-on in the school for novices. 'Her purpose is to undermine His Excellency's trust in you, and have the baby put in the orphanage,' she said. 'I think you should punish her, Mother. Otherwise who knows what the consequences would be for the child.'

The Mother Superior showed her scorn for Sister Ana with a smile. 'I cannot punish her,' she said. 'This is not a prison. You are all free to do what you wish as long as you do not break the rules of the Order.' She stopped and looked in the direction of the cradle to check whether the baby had woken up, then resumed: 'I have no doubt that His Excellency will see through her lunacy, but she could still cause a scandal that would ultimately hurt us. It is this I cannot allow. I do not want Lucía or you driving her to the city. Tell her that you are obeying my instructions.'

Sister Beatriz bowed. 'It was my duty to inform you, Reverend Mother.'

'You did the right thing, Beatriz.'

'The problem could be solved by sending her away.'

'There would have to be a formal inquest for that. I would have to write to the Superioress, who would then invite Ana and me to the capital to argue our case before her. You and the other sisters might have to give evidence too. It would be very unpleasant. Instead I am hoping that sooner or later Ana will go of her own accord.'

'The child's life may be in danger.'

Sister María Inés looked at the young nun with severity.

'What makes you think so?'

'She seems to be possessed without knowing it,' Sister Beatriz said. 'She goes round talking about demons.'

She added that in her opinion Sister Ana would not hesitate to act if she thought that she was serving God. The fact was that she doubted whether the baby was human, and therefore she might do something to free the convent of evil.

Sister María Inés listened, pouting. 'Does she plan to steal the baby? Is there anything else that you know?'

'I am only guessing. It's my impression from having talked to her.'

'I want you to carry on talking to her. Let me know everything she says.'

The other woman promised to do it. Then she asked: 'Will you let me help with the baby?'

They looked alike in their white habits and black veils and the rosaries looped over their belts. The child stirred in his sleep and the cradle rocked a little. Sister María Inés looked at him. Her life was devoted to love, but how much easier it was to love the whole world than a single human being. The latter was, in fact, forbidden to them; their vow of chastity even ruled out platonic love. She said: 'Very well. You can be responsible for his milk. I will show you how to prepare it. You should follow my directions carefully. Keep everything clean – hygiene is very important. Things that have no effect on our stomachs may seriously harm an infant.'

'How many times does he need to be fed?'

'The feeding I will do myself for the time being. You will be helping me. Also, you can wash his clothes and bed linen. I will still be changing and washing him myself unless I am occupied when all that needs to be done.'

'You should let me take him out. The sun will do him good. All that mould can't be good for him.'

'But keep him well wrapped. Be very careful he does not catch a cold.'

The child woke up at that moment and the Mother Superior went to pick him up. She came back and sat down, cradling him in her arms. The young nun touched his forehead with her fingertips.

'This is my private miracle, Beatriz,' the Mother Superior said. 'Never doubt God's goodness.'

The bell sounded for the midmorning prayer but, entranced by the child, neither of the women moved for a few moments. The young nun was first to notice, and told the Mother Superior, who, holding the child, followed her unwillingly to the chapel.

The punishment of the two nuns was perhaps not as severe as it could have been, considering Sister María Inés's fury. Nevertheless, it was unjust and hurtful enough to change the mood in the convent. Everybody still carried out their tasks with diligence, stopped their work every three hours to pray in the chapel, ate together in the refectory, but a shadow had fallen over whatever they did, and they had lost their cheerfulness. The Mother Superior noticed it and wondered whether perhaps she had treated the two nuns a bit too harshly, but did nothing to show her doubt. She neither called off their punishment nor moderated it, but hoped that the incident would soon be forgotten. A few days later, things were indeed beginning to return to normal, but then something happened that shattered any hope for peace between her and the sisters.

She had left Sister Beatriz in charge of the child and gone to midday prayer. When she returned to her room, she was pleased to find the young nun also kneeling in prayer, with the child on her lap and her head bowed. She had insisted that her assistant should not neglect her religious duties even when she had to care for the child, and had instructed her to recite the canonical hours wherever she happened to be with as much devotion as if she were in the chapel. The Mother Superior paused at the door and waited for the nun to finish. When Sister Beatriz crossed herself and stood up with the child in her arms, the Mother Superior shut the door. The young woman gave a start.

'I am very pleased with you, Beatriz,' the Mother Superior said. 'Your assistance with the child is important to me and your absence from the chapel has not turned you into a heathen.'

'I'm glad that I can be of help, Reverend Mother.'

'One day I hope to repay you for all your kindness and good sense.'

She stretched her arms towards the baby and the nun obediently handed him to her. Sister María Inés told her when to have his food ready. The young woman bowed and left the room. In recent days Sister María Inés had been feeling a drop in temperature. Autumn was coming and soon the weather would turn and something would have to be done about keeping the room warm. Winters in the convent were bitterly cold. In the past, she used to welcome them with penitent spirit, but now she had to think less about her soul and more about the child. She opened a drawer in her desk and took out the box where she kept her savings. She counted the money and decided to ask Sister Beatriz to buy her a small stove the next time she went to the city.

She wrapped the child well with a blanket and went out for a stroll before it was time to feed him. There was no one outside: it was the time when the nuns gathered round the refectory table to parcel the altar breads. Sister María Inés walked across the courtyard, observing everything as if she had never seen it before. The bell tower, the chimneys, the gargoyles on the roofs, the stork nests, the faces on the statues of the saints in the cloister, even the moss on the flagstones and the peeling paint on the old doors fascinated her. For her the signs of decay were not simply reminders of the passage of time but the telltale signs of an undying remorse that trailed back to the Fall of Man.

A stork rising from its nest caught her eye and she watched it fly away with a few easy flaps of its wings. The birds would soon be leaving for Africa. In a medieval bestiary that she had found in the convent library, she had read that if a stork's nest caught fire the bird would stay and burn in it rather than abandon it. She had no doubt that it was true and often wondered whether she herself would have the courage to do the same if it ever came to it. She wanted to be able to say that she would, but the choice she had made when she was young did not allow her to believe with certainty that she was capable of self-sacrifice.

At the refectory, she pushed open the heavy door just a crack and watched the nuns working. She could not hear what they were saying. She closed the door softly and walked on. Suddenly she had an idea and climbed the steps to the dormitory and walked along the loggia. There were no locks on the doors to the nuns' rooms, a tradition that dated back to the early days of the convent, when a strict mother superior used to pay un-announced visits in the middle of the night to ensure the sisters were not violating their vows in any way. Confident that the nuns were busy in the refectory and also that the wooden floor of the loggia would give her ample warning if anyone happened to come, Sister María Inés entered Sister Ana's room.

She never spied on the nuns, but this time she believed that she had to break her rule because the truth could be a matter of life and death. She paced round, holding the child in her arms. A strong smell of turpentine was trapped in the room, where the windows seemed not to have been opened in a long time. A canvas with an unfinished picture was on the easel. On a table in the middle of the room were painting brushes and knives, a large palette, many jars with pigments, a pestle and mortar. Sister María Inés did not know what she hoped to find – perhaps a diary, where Sister Ana had recorded her thoughts and evil plans, would be a good reason to expel her. She quickly admitted that her foe was too clever to make such simple mistakes. The gramo-phone was the only item that aroused her curiosity. She peeked inside its horn, gave the turntable a little push and flicked through the records of the language courses. On one of the covers it read:
. . . a truly natural way of learning a language, a way you first, as

a child, learned your own mother tongue. It was a confident statement printed in thick dark letters. She read on: *The results of this method are astonishing. Under this tireless tutor, mastery becomes easy . . .* As a child Sister María Inés remembered her father having an Edison phonograph that played wax cylinders – flat records had not become popular until some time after she had taken the veil. She put the gramophone records back exactly where she had found them and came out into the loggia again.

She had found no clue about Sister Ana's plans. Perhaps, she thought, despite what Sister Beatriz feared, Sister Ana had no plan at all – just hate that sooner or later would burn out. The sky was scattered with clouds that kept the air cool but blocked only a few sunrays. She felt that she ought to ask God forgiveness for having treated Sister Carlota and Sister Teresa harshly. She entered the chapel, where only a few inches of daylight crept in past the vestibule. A few things could be vaguely seen inside: the crucifix, the large candlesticks, the altar table. The nuns celebrated Mass every Sunday, against the rule which stated that only an ordained priest could administer the sacraments. The Bishop, who could only visit one Sunday a month, turned a blind eye on the understanding that the Mother Superior would not consecrate the host. She had promised him not to do it but had disobeyed, every time, convinced that it was far more important that the nuns received the Body of Christ than obey a rule which Sister María Inés was not even certain had a basis in the Holy Scripture. Against a wall was the confessional. She gave it a cursory glance, thinking that she would have to be careful what she would tell the Bishop about the child when he visited at the end of the month. Then she knelt in front of the tabernacle and bowed her head in prayer with the child in her arm, and her eyes shut. She said: 'O God, I have done wrong. I have been cruel to Carlota and Teresa. Please forgive me. All I want is to carry out Your wish and save this child. Only You know how important he is to me . . . I wish I could explain this to the sisters, but please help so that I do not have to do it. If I were expelled from the Order, it would be difficult for the child too.'

She felt a mounting determination and opened her eyes. She placed the child gently on the floor in front of her and continued: 'I have to be strong for this child. There are people who might hurt him whether they know what they are doing or not.' The child was looking up at her. She said: 'O God, give me the strength and wisdom . . .' She prayed a little longer and then crossed herself, picked up the child and stood up.

There was no one in the courtyard when she came out of the chapel. She glanced at the clock on the bell tower. There was still a little time before Sister Beatriz brought the child's milk to her room. Carefully she began to climb down the steps to the courtyard with the child still in her arms. Stretched out in the shade of the cloister, one of Sister Carlota's stray dogs raised its head and watched her. When she reached the bottom of the chapel steps, it stood up and began to cross the courtyard. Sister María Inés glanced at it. Then she looked down at the child and wrapped the blanket tightly round him.

As the dog came closer, it began to growl. 'Go,' the woman said. 'Go away.' The dog continued to growl at her. Sister María Inés squeezed the child in her arms and tried to kick the dog. She missed and the dog gave a bark. 'Go! Go!' she shouted and kicked out a few more times, her heart beating faster. The dog avoided her foot and snapped at her ankle. She backed off. The dog made a dart for her habit and tore a piece off the edge.

She kept her eyes fixed on the animal and took off her belt with her free hand. Her rosary fell to the ground but she made no attempt to pick it up. She wanted to go towards the chapel but the dog was in her way, so she backed towards the well in the middle of the courtyard, slowly winding the end of her belt round her hand. The dog continued to bark and show its teeth. She made a sudden attempt to hit it with her belt but missed, and it lunged at her. She quickly hit out again. This time the buckle found the dog's muzzle and the animal retreated with a yelp. She knew it would come back – it would not go away because of a little blood. She glanced behind her to see where the well was and she moved slowly backwards until she reached it. She had been holding the child with one arm for a long time and now felt a painful tightening of her muscles. But she did not loosen her hold. Then the child began to cry. She leaned against the well, breathing heavily, not taking her eyes off the dog, and rocked the child. She said: 'God help me. O God . . .'

The animal came cautiously towards her again, afraid of the belt but not prepared to give up. Out of the corner of her eye, Sister María Inés saw the door of the refectory open. One after another the nuns came out, but instead of going to her aid they watched with horror from the arches of the cloister. She felt the child slip from her, and the hand that held the belt moved instinctively to take some of the weight that until then was carried only by her other arm. Then the dog darted at her and bit her on the ankle. She felt the teeth clamp over the bone and immediately withdraw, leaving a wet sensation on her skin. She heard a nun scream: 'Mother of God! It will kill them both!' She guessed that it was Sister Beatriz. It was she. She tried to run to the Mother Superior but the other nuns held her back. Sister María Inés turned to the dog and struck it with the belt several times. While the dog retreated, she heard: 'Carlota, quick!' The old nun, who had just come from the kitchen, crossed the courtyard as fast as she could and took the dog by the scruff of its neck.

In the middle of the courtyard, Sister María Inés stood with the crying child. Her arms shook and her ankle was bleeding but she seemed not to know it. When the nuns approached her, she threatened them with her belt and they quickly backed off. They watched her limp across the courtyard with the child in her arms, breathing heavily, and they instantly knew that from that moment on there was no power on earth or in heaven that could make her heart good again.

Over the years Sister Carlota had given shelter to many dogs in the convent. Almost every time she went to the city, which was three or four times a year, she came back with a starving mongrel that she had found wandering the streets. Moved by her kindness, the Mother Superior let her keep them as long as they did not get in the way of the old nun's duties. Sister Carlota washed every new arrival with soapy water, healed their wounds with mercurochrome and their mange with sulphurated lime, and ended the ritual by putting a small wooden cross round their neck, engraved with a name she had chosen from the Bible. Treated with such care, the dogs gave her their absolute loyalty. They never barked in her presence; they ran to her when they heard their names and followed her everywhere apart from the chapel, where she had taught them to wait at the door while she prayed with the sisters. They slept anywhere in the convent, under the arches of the cloister, on the steps of the chapel, in the abandoned buildings, depending on the weather. Sister Carlota fed them with whatever she could spare from the meagre provisions of the convent and the bones and offal she was given for free in the city, but it was hardly enough to satisfy their appetites, and every morning she took to letting them out to forage like wild animals in the woods round the convent.

On one of her rare holidays some years earlier, she had visited the famous Cimetière des Chiens near Paris, where a monument to a Saint Bernard dog gave her the idea to train her dogs to rescue people lost in the sierra. When she returned to the convent, she spoke to the Mother Superior. Sister María Inés doubted that Sister Carlota's strays could match the abilities of the noble Swiss breed but did not want to disappoint the nun and gave her consent. As she suspected, it was a futile endeavour. The dogs were too old to learn and nothing could make them relinquish the freedom to which they had been accustomed. Sister Carlota tried to teach them discipline, but even though they wanted to please her they were unable to understand her orders and simply looked at her with eyes full of curiosity. She threatened to beat them, but they could sense that she would not do it. She hid things and showed them how to find them, but they had no natural drive for searching unless it was food they were after. And so, with great disappointment, she acknowledged her failure and let them do whatever God intended them to do.

At night the nuns were often awoken by the sound of a dog howling, which was then joined by the howls of a second dog, then another, and so on, until the whole convent echoed with their cries. Then Sister Carlota had to get out of bed and search in the dark until she had found every dog and calmed them all down. It was not her only problem. She also had to put up with their untamed bowels, which they emptied with abandon. She rushed to clean after them, puzzling over how they were capable of turning out such an unimaginable amount of excrement when they seemed to eat so little. Worse still was their fondness for vice, which scandalised the old nun and made her question Noah's wisdom in having taken them on the Ark. And yet, whatever their filthy and dissolute habits, they had never until now been aggressive towards anyone.

After the attack Sister María Inés returned to her room and sat rocking the child. Sister Beatriz came with the bowl of milk and did not want to leave. The Mother Superior sent her away, reassuring her: 'Do not worry. The child has not been harmed. He is only scared. It was not as frightening as it seemed.' But as she fed him, put him in the cradle and rocked him to sleep, she could not stop shaking with fear. Finally, she sat on the edge of her bed and began to calm down. On the floor a few drops of blood marked her course from the door when she had first come in. She found her belt and put it on, noticing that her rosary was missing. She had no idea where she could have lost it. For a moment she wondered whether the incident meant that she had lost God's support but dismissed her fears. She thought that God ought to be pleased that she had saved an innocent life.

She lifted the hem of her habit and inspected her wound with a nurse's detachment. Her fingers traced the blood that was beginning to congeal. The marks left by the dog's teeth were deep but the wound did not need stitching. She was not bothered by the likelihood of a scar. She cleaned the wound with water, then with surgical spirit and finally wrapped it with a clean cloth. She did everything with competence and the composure of one who has seen far greater horrors in her life. Then she lay in bed and rested until she heard the bell. She was too tired to leave her room and for the first time in all her years in the convent she did not go to the chapel for prayer but knelt and said the angelus instead. In the evening, when she brought her some soup, Sister Beatriz found her kneeling by her bed again. The Mother Superior finished her prayer and stood up. She said: 'Thank you, but I am not hungry.'

Sister Beatriz put the dish on the desk. 'You have to eat, Mother. Who knows what would've happened today if you hadn't been so strong.'

The nun stood beside the cradle and observed the sleeping child. The Mother Superior sat to eat. 'I am now convinced that he would be lost without me,' she said.

Sister Beatriz put her hand in her pocket and took out a dusty rosary. She brushed it against her habit and gave it to the other woman. The Mother Superior took it with both hands, touched

97

the cross to her lips with great relief and looped the worn string of beads over her belt. She had been given it when she was a postulant and expected that she would be buried with it wound round her fingers. Over the years she had attended several burials, sometimes leading the funeral service from the altar, feeling no fear but standing in awe of the start of the eternal life. The open coffin on the bier, the dead nun dressed in a starched habit, recumbent with her hands clasped in prayer on her chest, the ashen face which a little earlier stirred with the vestiges of life – they always seemed to her to exude the calm of a great burden having been lifted. Sitting now at her desk, she felt the smell of burning candles and the words of the funeral Mass came into her mind: *Requiem aeternam dona eis, Domine, et lux perpetua luceat eis* – Eternal rest give to them, Lord, and let perpetual light shine upon them . . .

'How is your ankle, Reverend Mother?' the nun asked.

'You can help me change the bandage.'

She left her soup unfinished and lay down on the bed, pointing at the surgical spirit, the cotton wool and some clean cloths on the table. The young nun began to unwrap the cloth tied round Sister María Inés's ankle. The Mother Superior said: 'Only clean the wound with alcohol. If it turns out that I need treatment, it will have to be a vaccine. But I do not think the dog carries rabies.'

The nun soaked a piece of cotton wool in surgical spirit and began to clean the wound. 'Such a thing has never happened before,' she said. She cleaned the wound a second time and began to wrap a clean cloth round the swollen ankle. 'Sister Carlota is very sorry, She wants to come and see you.'

'I want to see no one.'

Sister Beatriz finished attending to the wound and gathered

the used cotton wool and the dirty bandage to throw away. The Mother Superior covered her ankles again with her habit and glanced at the sleeping child from where she lay. She said: 'I want you to stay with the child tomorrow, Beatriz. You will have to miss the early morning prayer.'

The nun bowed and went out with one last glance at the child. For a long time afterwards, Sister María Inés was unable to sleep. When she finally fell asleep, she dreamed that it was the time of prayer and she was on her way to the chapel. But when she climbed the steps and dipped her fingers in the marble stoup next to the door, she found it empty. She quickly went to the well to fill the bucket, but the well was dry. When she returned to the chapel, the Virgin was standing at the door. Sister María Inés crossed herself and tried to walk past but the Virgin stopped her. She said: 'You have to cleanse yourself of your sins first, Isabel.' The nun did not know what to do. Then the Virgin closed the door and the prayer began inside the chapel. Sister María Inés went away . . .

She woke with the sound of the bell at dawn, still shaken by her dream, and the first thing she did was to check that the child was well. Then she washed her face and sat at her desk, which was what she always did when she had to make a difficult decision. For a while she wavered, but then she called to mind the incident with the dog in all its horror and had no doubt about what she ought to do. Someone knocked on her door. She expected it to be Sister Beatriz but it was Sister Carlota. The Mother Superior looked at her coolly.

'I wanted to see you, Reverend Mother,' the elderly nun said. 'I'm very sorry about what happened. I will have the dogs neutered. It will calm them down.'

'That will not be necessary.'

There was a knock on the door and Sister Beatriz entered with the bowl of milk for the child and a walking stick for the Mother Superior.

'It was a mistake to give sanctuary to those animals,' Sister María Inés said. 'But I do not blame you, Carlota. You did it out of kindness.'

As soon as the old nun was gone, the Mother Superior sat on the edge of the bed and replaced the bandage herself: the wound was healing well. When she finished, she unlocked the cupboard where she kept the rat poison. Sister Beatriz watched her. 'Feed the child,' the Mother Superior said and took the poison and the walking stick. 'I will not be long.' The young nun followed the Mother Superior with her eyes until she left the room.

The idea had come to Sister María Inés during the night, and once she had decided no one could dissuade her from going through with it. Leaning on the walking stick, she went downstairs. There was no one around: the sisters were in the chapel. She went across the cloister with the bag of poison under her arm, her walking stick tapping against the flagstones. The offal for the dogs was kept in the buttery. She took several pieces and went round the convent calling them. They came briskly from several directions, wagging their tails. Sister María Inés was ready to use the walking stick to protect herself but the dogs were as friendly as they had always been. She was uncertain which one had attacked her but it did not matter. After counting them to make certain they were all there, she dipped the meat in the arsenic, taking care not to touch the powder with her fingers. The dogs smelled the meat and crowded round her. She said: 'Be patient. There is enough for all of you.' She threw them the pieces and they ate hungrily. When she had thrown all the meat, she sat on a bench in the cloister and watched the dogs eat. She had no doubt that what she had done was necessary to keep the child safe.

Later, when the prayer ended and the nuns came out, they could tell right away that the dogs were in the courtyard. But, it being dark inside the chapel, it took the women's eyes some time to get used to the daylight and only then did they see that the dogs lying in the dust were not lazing in the sun, as they had at first assumed, but were in fact slowly dying in the creamy pools of their own vomit.

The chair was placed beside one of the tall windows and the velvet drapes were parted to let in the noontime sunlight. The barber shook the gown a few times and tied it again round Bishop Estrada's neck. Then he took his scissors and comb from the breast pocket of his smock and resumed his work. Somewhere in the room, a clock struck twelve in an unhurried, melodic way. The Bishop stared out of the window and sighed.

'Are you perhaps too warm, Your Excellency?' the barber asked.

'I am fine, Alfredo. Thank you.'

'Would you like a glass of water?'

The barber poured a glass from the jug on the table and handed it to his customer with a deferential bow. Bishop Estrada took a sip out of politeness and gave it back. 'Let us continue, Alfredo. I am afraid I have a very busy schedule today.'

The vast room began to echo again with the sound of the scissors as more tufts of hair dropped to the marble floor.

'Your hair is a wonderful colour, Your Excellency. It couldn't have been a more perfect silver.'

'Euphemisms are unnecessary, Alfredo,' the Bishop said. 'It is grey.'

'With your permission, I don't agree. And the roots are very healthy. I bet you haven't lost a single hair since you were born.'

'I don't know,' the Bishop said indifferently. 'I haven't counted them.'

'Oh, it's evident. Men much younger than you already suffer from galloping baldness.'

'You talk about it as if it were consumption, Alfredo.'

'It is a threat to my profession, Your Excellency.'

'Maybe you barbers should go back to being the barber surgeons of old times,' the Bishop said.

But it was true that his hair, which was thick like a boy's, his Roman forehead, his blue eyes and lean figure were his consolation against the cruelties of ageing, which he had begun to notice when he had turned fifty. While the barber worked, the Bishop's gaze wandered about the room. Its grandeur recalled the absolute clerical authority of another era. The walls were hung with the portraits of his predecessors going back several centuries, while above the double doors, through which the visitors were admitted to the room, was his episcopal coat of arms. Several other smaller doors led to his secretaries' offices as well as his private quarters, where he could come and go unseen by his visitors and staff. In the middle of the room, facing the double doors, was a big desk of varnished oak scattered with the paperwork which was a permanent obstacle to Bishop Estrada's fulfilling his true pastoral duties. The barber pushed his customer's head a little to trim his sideburn and said: 'It seems we are enjoying an Indian summer, Your Excellency.'

'It would appear so.'

'It arrived right on time. San Miguel's feast is tomorrow. One wonders how it keeps falling on the same day year after year. It is a very interesting meteorological phenomenon.'

The Bishop did not resist the temptation to correct him. 'Last year it was on San Martín's day. Eleventh of November.'

'You have a superb memory, Your Excellency.'

The Bishop heard the double doors open and recognised his deacon's footsteps. 'What is it, Ignacio?' he asked without turning round.

The deacon, a very young man in a black habit, clasped his

hands and spoke with a flawless diction: 'There is someone here to see you, Your Excellency.'

'Who is it?'

'She has no appointment. I tried to tell her that it is not possible without an appointment but she insists. She says it is a matter of great urgency.'

'A woman?'

'A *sister*, Your Excellency – from the convent of Our Lady of Mercy.'

The Bishop was silent for a moment. 'Very well,' he said. 'Tell her to wait.'

The deacon bowed in silence and closed the door.

'Are we done, Alfredo?' the Bishop asked the barber. 'You are not building the Great Wall of China.'

The barber quickly finished his haircut without making any more small talk and handed the Bishop a mirror to hear his verdict. Bishop Estrada looked at his reflection fleetingly. 'Very good, Alfredo. Thank you.' The barber bowed, removed the gown from the Bishop's neck and brushed the hairs off his black cassock. As an apology for having rushed him, Bishop Estrada paid him more than usual. The barber made an even deeper bow, swept the floor and left with his tools and the dustpan. For a while the Bishop paced the room, looking at his reflection in the marble floor, until his random orbit brought him to the window, where he stood with his hands clasped behind his back. During the sixteenth century the city had gone through a period of economic splendour thanks to the textile, jewellery and leather industries, but then had entered into decline under the Bourbon rule. At the beginning of the nineteenth century the French occupation and the Carlist disputes, which followed the war of independence, had impoverished its economy even further. The Bishop had arrived when it was still a poor city, but in recent years a steady growth of wealth had turned it into a busy centre for commerce with an abundant market that drew crowds from beyond the borders of the diocese. The old horse-drawn carts that used to move slowly down the cobbled streets had now to make way for petrol cars that went past at top speed and disappeared from view before one had time to put a curse on them.

Why a brilliant man with a great future like Bishop Ezequiel Estrada would choose a provincial diocese was a mystery to everyone who met him. Impressed by his intelligence and credentials, they could only interpret his choice in terms of his humility, which was evident despite the splendour of his episcopal ring, his pectoral cross and elegant cassock. His diocese consisted of several hundred thousand faithful, hundreds of priests, a well-attended seminary and many monasteries and convents, which made great demands on his time and strength. Nevertheless, he considered that his main obligation was preaching and made a point of visiting every parish at least once every fifth year, even the smaller ones in the mountains where his car could not go and he could only get to by horse. He was not in favour of building new churches or restoring the old ones but insisted on using the funds to help the poor this side of the grave. He had also reformed the curriculum of the seminary, adding more science courses and a physical-education class whose syllabus was based on the Swedish light-gymnastics system, for it was obvious to him that a priest needed to be fit to spread God's word.

These were the enthusiastic innovations of a man who was aware of his calling from a young age. However, his father, a marquis who was descended from one of the oldest and most illustrious families in the country, had pressed him to pursue a legal career and he had obeyed. When he obtained his doctorate in law at the age of twenty-three, he finally asked permission from his father to study for the priesthood. The marquis reluctantly agreed on the condition that he would carry out his theological studies not at home but in Rome, so that he would not end up as a village priest or provincial monsignor. The following year Ezequiel entered Collegio Capranica. After he was ordained a priest, he continued his studies, specialising in ecclesiastical diplomacy, in which he excelled. As part of their coursework, the students were required to give seminars that were attended by cardinals and other high members of the Curia, and it was there that he was noticed by an influential cardinal who offered him a position in the diplomatic service of the Vatican. During the time that he held that post, he had coordinated the relief effort for an epidemic of yellow fever in West Africa, and it was in one of his visits there that he had first met Sister María Inés. Several years later, when he became a bishop, they renewed their acquaintance, which, over time, developed into a good friendship.

He picked up a silver hand bell from his desk and rang it. A moment later the door opened and Sister Ana came in. Bishop Estrada had not expected to see her. She was one of the people he least cared for, even though he had long guessed her great adoration of him. She strode across the room with a parcel under her arm and kissed his ring, kneeling with excessive reverence. The Bishop was annoyed. 'Please, Sister,' he said. 'Stand up. You are not having an audience with His Holiness.'

He showed her to the chair near the window where he had had his haircut and fetched another from across the room. The nun observed him with an awe that always made him ill at ease.

'Thank you for taking the time to see me, Your Excellency,' she said. 'I know how busy you are.'

'I am always glad to see you, Sister,' the Bishop replied with carefully judged civility. 'I am indeed very busy.' And he pointed at the piled folders on his desk.

'Oh, I understand. Paperwork must be a heavy cross to bear.'

The overstatement made Bishop Estrada feel uncomfortable. He said: 'It is only a paper cross. I should not be complaining.'

He looked at her without blinking, despite the bright sunlight, and tried to guess the reason for her visit. She had never come to his office before. They met in the convent, and although she was always deferential to him she did not seem to join in the frivolity of his lunches with the nuns. Then he remembered that she had once spoken to him outside confession about certain grievances she had had against the Mother Superior. He had thought her bitterness inappropriate for a nun but had said nothing. Seated beside the window, he now expected her to talk to him about the same matter again, but Sister Ana handed him her parcel. 'I meant to give you this for Christmas, Your Excellency,' she said. 'But I confess I could not wait that long.'

The Bishop was surprised, although he often received presents. He said: 'Sister Ana, you never struck me as the kind of person who subscribes to the necessity of this practice.' Not wanting to appear ungrateful, he quickly untied the string and unfolded the brown paper under the nun's stare. 'Anyway, I thank you . . . Ah!' he exclaimed. 'The Transfiguration. Why, it is delightful, Sister.' He held it up to the light and admired its details.

'Do you really like it, Your Excellency?'

Bishop Estrada attempted a light-hearted comparison: 'It is on a par with the Raphael painting in the Vatican.'

'I knew you would notice it,' the nun said, beaming with delight. 'It is an exact copy. Of course, my colours are poor in comparison, but everything else is more or less right.'

'More or less,' the Bishop said. 'Yes.'

The upper half of the painting showed the Transfiguration on Mount Tabor. Christ, Moses and Elijah were floating in the air in front of a big illuminated cloud, while below them several figures prostrated themselves in homage. In the lower part of the painting, the Apostles were attempting to free a possessed boy of his demon but could not do it without Christ's help. Bishop Estrada continued to study the painting. 'The shading . . . the folds in the clothes . . . the landscape in the distance . . . all exquisite,' he said. 'How long did it take you?'

'Oh, a few weeks here and there, Your Excellency.'

She had worked on it, in fact, for three months with a dedication that was as intense and unyielding as her devotion to God. On weekdays she got up very early, without having set her alarm clock, to do as much work as she could until the bell rang for dawn prayer. Shaking from the cold in the unheated room, she put on her black cape and a pair of knitted gloves, and sat to prepare the paints according to the instructions found in Renaissance recipes: terre verte for the flesh tones, azurite for Christ's mantle, brown ochre for the earth. Then she had to leave. During the day she stole a few minutes to come to her room and add a few dabs of paint to her canvas, but the real work was done in the evenings, when she stood at her easel in the lamplight until the Great Silence began. Then she cleaned her brushes and, giddy from the turpentine vapours, eyes smarting, fingers stiff, she knelt down to thank God for her talent before going to sleep. On Sundays she painted all day, stopping only to go to prayer or to join the sisters at lunch, and then hurried back to her room, where her painting was starting to dry. In order to avoid any distraction, she worked with the windows closed until she was about to faint from the smell of the pigments. Reluctantly, she opened the windows and resumed her work while the happy voices of the sisters chatting outside made her feel like an exile from the Garden of Eden.

She now said: 'I wanted very much to ask you to sit for one

of the Apostles, Your Excellency. But I was afraid you would refuse.'

'I would have been honoured, Sister. But I would still have refused in all humility, I am afraid.'

The Bishop continued to study the painting with an amiable expression, pointing from time to time at a detail and asking a question. She answered with more words than were necessary and he listened, nodding, while his eyes roved over the canvas. Finally he put the painting down and said: 'Well, thank you for this, Sister. It was truly a wonderful surprise.'

'I am glad that you like it, Your Excellency. But I am afraid I have not come only for that.'

'Oh, you didn't,' the Bishop said and his face darkened. 'Is there something else?'

'I felt it my duty to inform you about a very serious situation that has arisen in the convent.'

'Is this about your dispute with the Mother Superior again?'

'No, Your Excellency. This time it is something even more serious. It's about the orphan.'

The Bishop frowned. 'What orphan?'

'The Devil sent him. I am convinced – even if the child is innocent himself.'

Bishop Estrada began to lose his patience. 'Please tell me what you have come to tell me.'

The nun blushed and quickly told him about the recent events in the convent. While she spoke, the Bishop paced the room listening attentively without attempting to interrupt her. She said: 'I hope you agree that it is inappropriate for a child to live in the convent, Your Excellency.'

The Bishop did not share her lack of sympathy but did not want to say so. 'It is certainly unusual,' he said. 'The Mother Superior's intentions are admirable. But you are right, Sister.

She should not make such a serious decision on her own.' Then he dismissed the nun's suggestions of satanic involvement with an unhappy smile, adding: 'But in any case, I do not believe the poor thing is the spawn of Satan. The demon is inside those who choose to abandon their own children like that. Thank you for letting me know. You did the right thing.'

The nun bowed. 'I would have come sooner, Your Excellency, but I am virtually held prisoner.'

'Prisoner? What do you mean, Sister?'

'The Mother Superior has ordered that I am not to be given a lift to the city. But I managed to hide in the van of the baker who collects our altar breads.'

'Was that deceit really necessary?'

'Oh, you should see her, Your Excellency. She has changed since the coming of the child.'

'Are you talking about Sister María Inés?'

'She poisoned the dogs which Sister Carlota looked after. It was terrible,' the woman said and described how the nuns had found the dogs dying in the courtyard.

The Bishop was shocked but tried not to show it. He said: 'I always thought those dogs were a nuisance – not to mention the issue of hygiene. Couldn't that be the reason for their extermination?'

'No, Your Excellency. She believed they were a threat to the child. Sister Carlota is deeply upset.'

'Why did Sister María Inés think the dogs might attack the child?'

'There was an incident recently . . . Having witnessed it, I personally think it was blown out of proportion. The Mother has lost her reason.

The Bishop looked away and quoted Terence: '*I am human and nothing that is human is alien to me.*'

'I implore you to intervene before something much worse happens,' the nun said.

Bishop Estrada stood at the window with his hands clasped and thought for a moment. 'Very well,' he said. 'I am very busy over the next few days. But I promise to come to the convent before the end of the week.'

This time he offered her his hand without qualms about his humility. The nun kissed his ring and bowed. The Bishop said nothing more but followed her with his unsettled eyes as she crossed the room towards the door, gliding silently over the marble floor like the ghosts he sometimes saw in the languor of his siesta.

Bishop Estrada had surprised everyone when he had announced that he was to become confessor to the nuns of Our Lady of Mercy himself instead of appointing a priest from his diocese. The post had fallen vacant when the elderly priest who visited the convent once a week had died of exhaustion during his pilgrimage to the cathedral of Santiago de Compostela. Months had passed without the nuns celebrating Mass and confessing their sins. Sister María Inés had written to the Bishop several times but received no reply. Then, exasperated with ecclesiastical bureaucracy, she started to say Mass every Sunday herself, against the rules of the Church.

For his part, the Bishop was too busy with other affairs, and the request from the convent in the sierra had slipped his mind. After showing him the first couple of letters from the Mother Superior, his secretary stopped trying to draw his attention to them, in the belief that he was well aware of the matter and would settle it in due course. The deacon filed them away, something he did as a matter of course, for there was such a constant flood of letters from every corner of the diocese, with invitations, requests, awards, threats, petitions for canonisation and appeals to the Church's charity, that it was impossible to answer every single one of them. When months later the letters from the Mother Superior continued to arrive, the deacon risked the impertinence of reminding his superior about them. Bishop Estrada admitted his mistake, criticised his secretary for his excessive deference and ordered that a priest be found immediately. In the meantime he visited the convent to apologise to the nuns in person.

It was a Sunday when he drove there in his Model T Ford, the same car he would later give as a gift to the nuns. He had only visited the convent once before, during one of his regular whistle-stop tours of the diocese. He parked his car at the entrance, brushed the dust off his coat, took off his gloves, his goggles and the leather helmet that made him look like an aviator and climbed the steps. He was about to ring the doorbell when he heard chanting. Guessing that he had arrived at the time of prayer, he decided not to disturb the nuns. Instead he pushed the heavy door and walked quietly across the cloistered path with the intention of killing time until they had finished.

On his brief previous visit he had paid little attention to the convent, which now struck him as a marvellous place. Time and damp had scarred the saints in the niches beyond recognition; the worn flagstones shone from thousands of feet having trodden on them over the centuries; the wooden staircases groaned under his weight, while on the tall chimneys storks kept watch over the convent. He did not dare enter the abandoned buildings, which seemed to him in such a bad state that they might collapse at any moment, but looked in through the broken windows and felt the cool draught blowing through the rooms which stirred up the dust on the floor and formed it into peculiar shapes. In the garden he wandered among the flowerbeds, where the fragrant air swarmed with insects that scattered ahead of his flapping cassock. Everything, even the ruins, agreed with his idea of what a convent should be: a place neither on earth nor in heaven but at the exact midpoint between the two. With this thought in mind, he retraced his steps to the cloister and crossed the courtyard to have a drink of water from the well. It was while drinking from his cupped hands that he paid attention to the voices coming from the chapel and recognised not the words of the midmorning prayer, as he had assumed at first, but those of the Sunday Mass: *Gloria in excelsis Deo, et in terra pax hominibus bonae voluntatis* . . . Bishop Estrada wiped his hands and went to the chapel, where he stood at the door, his tall figure and black cassock obscuring the light. The Mother Superior recognised him immediately and stopped in the middle of the hymn.

'Please, Sisters,' the Bishop said. 'Carry on with the service.'

The nuns followed him with their eyes. The Mother Superior resumed the Gloria with a hesitant voice, her heart still palpitating with fear: '*Tu solus Altissimus, Jesu Christe, cum Sancto Spiritu, in gloria Dei Patris. Amen.*'

When the hymn ended, the Bishop gathered the skirt of his cassock and sat on a pew a few rows behind the nuns to attend the rest of the Mass. The Mother Superior completed the Canon and moved on to the Communion. At the back of the chapel the Bishop glared but did not interrupt her. He stayed in his seat, his hands clasped on his lap, his lips pouting, observing the nuns who knelt on the steps of the altar to receive the host: '*Corpus Domini nostri Jesu Christi custodiat animam tuam in vitam aeternam.*' When the nuns returned to their pews, the Mother Superior waited for the Bishop to come forward and receive the host too, but he did not move. She returned to the altar and concluded the Mass.

Afterwards Bishop Estrada waited for her at the door of the chapel. Sister María Inés kissed his ring and welcomed him to their convent. She said: 'If we knew you were coming, Your Excellency, we would have waited for you to lead the service.'

The Bishop gave her an ambiguous smile. 'Yes,' he said. 'My intention was to surprise you, Sister, but you surprised me instead.'

She understood. 'I admit my breaking the rules, Your Excellency, but you left us no choice.'

'You are right to be annoyed. I do not mind you having said Mass under the circumstances. As a matter of fact, you did it very well. But consecrating the host was wrong.'

'I promise you it will not happen again,' the woman said. 'But you ought to give us your word too that you will appoint a priest to our convent.'

The Bishop said what had been in his mind since his stroll around the convent: 'I have, Sister. Here is your priest.'

'You, Your Excellency?'

'I can only do one Sunday a month, I am afraid. Take it or leave it.'

'Will we be able to celebrate Mass the rest of the Sundays ourselves?'

The Bishop thought for a moment. 'I should not condone it,' he said. 'But promise me not to consecrate the Host again and we are agreed.'

And so he began to visit the convent. He looked forward to the last Sunday of the month, which he set aside for that purpose, despite having to leave the city early in the morning and the arduous drive on the unpaved road that climbed steeply up the hills and brought him, an hour and many twists and turns through the dense pine forest later, to his destination. As soon as Sister María Inés heard the engine of the Ford, she came to the door of the convent to wait for him and exchange the obligatory greetings. Then she showed him to his room, where he washed himself with the attention of one performing his ablutions, lay on the bed in his cassock and shut his eyes for a moment. Ten minutes was enough time for him to recover his strength and clerical authority. When the bell rang, he changed into his liturgical vestments, which he kept in a small suitcase of genuine cordovan leather, and made his way to the chapel, where the women were waiting.

Before the service he listened to confessions. Every time he sat in the cubicle, which had been made in medieval times, when people were much smaller, he felt a morbid sensation, for its size and smell of oak reminded him of a coffin. He continued to use it with bravery, saying nothing to anybody out of shame, since those who have true faith in God have no reason to fear death. After all, the use of the confessional was not symbolic: he could not tell with certainty who was on the other side of the lattice from the sound of their voice.

Although the nuns' sins were harmless, he often wondered whether the world had become more evil with time, which was how it seemed to him. Perhaps it was only the fact that his ability to tolerate cruelty had diminished with age. A few years earlier, at the time of the Moroccan war, an army lieutenant had come to see him with an unusual request: a soldier of the Spanish Legion had deserted and returned home but had then been arrested and sentenced to death. His last wish was to confess not to any priest but to the Bishop himself.

'Of course, you don't have to come if it inconveniences you in any way, Your Excellency,' the officer said. 'But granting a condemned man's wish is a tradition that is good to uphold. It makes the army seem a little more merciful – even towards those who don't deserve its mercy.'

'Is the man religious?'

'I doubt it, Your Excellency. Can a man who's betrayed his country be a good Christian?'

'*Render unto Caesar the things which are Caesar's,*' the Bishop said. 'One does not preclude the other.'

'Perhaps he had a change of heart,' the officer conceded. 'Someone with his prospects would be wise to do so.'

The man was held in a neighbouring town which Bishop Estrada had visited many times in the past, but it was his first time inside the barracks. Arranged around a cobbled courtyard, the buildings dated from the previous century and reminded the Bishop of a monastery: the same neatness, the same austerity, the same silence, the presence of men dressed alike. The only thing out of place was the tall perimeter wall with corbelled turrets where armed soldiers stood guard. The lieutenant greeted the Bishop and showed him to the prison. The smell of damp, the darkness, the same fear of enclosed spaces the Bishop would later suffer in the confessional of the convent of Our Lady of Mercy made him feel faint. Finally the officer stopped in front of a cell door and put the key in the lock, but did not turn it. He said: 'You can stay as long as you like, Your Excellency. Or we could go back right away and let him burn in Hell.'

The Bishop, ashamed and ashen-faced by his claustrophobia, replied in a hoarse voice: 'That is not for us to decide. Unlock the door.'

The interior of the cell was only lit by a shaft of sunlight coming through the barred window. A man lying on a bed that was too small for him spoke up: 'So you came.'

The Bishop took an uncertain step into the cell. The door swung shut behind him and the rasp of the lock made him uneasy. He asked: 'How are you, my son?'

The man chuckled: 'Oh, capital.'

There was another bed in the cell, and the Bishop sat down on it. He asked: 'Why did you ask expressly for me?'

'Parish priests are unable to carry on a conversation. They just recite bits from the Bible. If Rome ever ran out of priests it would start to train parrots.'

'Well, I am not a parrot,' Bishop Estrada said. 'What do you want to talk about?'

He stayed longer than he had expected, discussing religion with the condemned man, who had a very good knowledge of matters of faith. When the time came to leave, he was sorry to break off their conversation and promised to return. He visited the legionnaire every afternoon, sacrificing his siesta to debate, under the shadow of death and with a passion he had not felt since his student days: doctrinal issues, the sanctity of human life, Galileo's trial, Darwin's theory and other matters that divided the Church. Bishop Estrada marvelled at his opponent's intelligence. He could tell that the legionnaire was an educated man but only managed to make him admit this after he threatened not to come back. The man relented: 'I was once a priest, Your Excellency.'

Then Bishop Estrada saw him for what he really was, not simply the worthy opponent of their afternoon debates or the nameless soldier who had abandoned his post in a colonial war, but as a young man full of life who was about to die. From then on the Bishop tried everything to reverse the legionnaire's sentence and save him from death. He contacted everyone he knew and spoke with lawyers and the judges of the court martial, but they could not help. He travelled to the capital and asked for an audience with King Alfonso, who a few years later would flee the country and live the rest of his life in a hotel in Rome, but was turned down despite his family connections. In his desperation he wrote to the Holy Father, and some time later received a handwritten reply worthy of a Caesar, which sealed the condemned man's fate: *My dear Ezequiel, you are embarrassing us with a sentimentality that does not befit a senior member of our Church.*

On the day before the execution, Bishop Estrada came to the prison in the afternoon, as always, and saw the legionnaire for the last time. When the man asked him what they should discuss that day, the Bishop, astonished by the condemned man's composure, waved his hand: 'No, nothing today.' At dawn, when the black cockerel of the regiment began to crow, the Bishop returned to give the prisoner absolution and the viaticum with a trembling hand. He insisted that he was present at the execution despite the lieutenant's repeated attempts to dissuade him, and he walked at the side of the man reciting the Apostles' Creed until the officer put his hand on his shoulder. Bishop Estrada stopped and shot him an irritated glance: 'What do you want?'

'You can't go any further, Your Excellency. You would be in the line of fire.'

They had reached the place of execution. Standing aside, with horror in his eyes, Bishop Estrada continued to recite until the discharge of the firing squad. He never administered the last rites to a condemned man again. He did not discuss his feelings with anyone nor did he let his bitterness poison his respect for the Vatican. He maintained his pretence of authority, tried to regain his good humour for which he was known across the diocese and some time afterwards resumed his siestas. But his afternoons in bed were no longer peaceful. Everything bothered him: the ticking of the alarm clock on his bedside table, the springs of the mattress, the heat if the windows were shut, the draught if they were open. From time to time he thought that he saw ghosts in the room but kept their presence secret from everyone, telling himself that it was merely the curtains flapping. Still, he continued to live with the hope of finding sanctuary from the cruelty of the world, and then, years later, he happened to visit the convent of Our Lady of Mercy, where he believed that he had found the peace he was searching for.

The killing of the dogs plunged the convent into gloom. Even Sister Teresa, who did not like animals and considered them responsible for the spread of all kinds of disease, was stunned by the cruel act and feared for the future. She had no doubt that there would be repercussions but could not guess what they might be. When the nuns had walked out of the chapel, they had seen the dogs lying in the courtyard and had realised to their horror that they were dying and there was nothing that they could do. They had simply stood there, horrified, listening to the dogs yowling until Sister Carlota, always the last out of the door because of her old age, had come up behind them. Then the other women had emerged from their trance but had had no courage to tell her. They stood aside and let her pass without a word, and she, still unaware of the tragedy, thanked them for their good manners, lifted her habit a little, so as not to trip, and climbed down the steps to the courtyard. At the bottom of the steps her weak eyes finally alerted her to the fact that something strange was happening. When she understood what it was, she let out a loud cry and dropped to the ground. The sisters carried her to her room, put her in bed and stayed with her for the rest of the day, not leaving her even to go to the chapel but praying in the room instead.

In the morning the yowling stopped and the nuns knew that the dogs were finally dead. They used a wheelbarrow to carry them, a few at a time, to a clearing in the woods far from any stream, so as not to contaminate the water, and took turns digging a pit several feet deep where they threw them in and covered them with quicklime. Back in the convent they poured water over the dusty courtyard, which was stained with vomit and blood, and swept away the remains of the abominable act which the sun had not yet dried.

All that time Sister María Inés watched them from her room. She had done her duty, but it did not stop her from feeling sorry for Sister Carlota. She wanted to see her and explain the reasons for her action, but put it off for several days, afraid her visit might upset the woman even more. She gave the nuns a bottle of valerian pills with the instruction to give Carlota one every few hours, and enquired after her health every morning and afternoon until the old woman began to recover. Only then did she go to see her.

Dressed in her habit, Sister Carlota was lying in bed. Her eyes were fixed on the wall, her hands were holding the rosary and she was so still that for a moment Sister María Inés feared with a pang of guilt that the old woman was dead. Finally, Sister Carlota turned her head and gave her a glance that calmed the Mother Superior's fears but also made her regret having come. 'Ah, Carlota,' she said. 'How are you?'

The nun stared at her.

'I am glad you are feeling better, Carlota. I was worried about you. Did the valerian help?'

'You are not welcome here,' the old nun said.

'You should start coming to prayer again. It will do you good to leave your room.'

'I won't join one who worships the Devil.'

'Be careful, Carlota. Do not let your feelings for those dogs cloud your reason.'

'Sister Ana was right. You are possessed. Only God can help us now.'

The Mother Superior went crimson. She said: 'I tolerated your love of animals because it seemed harmless to me. But I was proved wrong.'

The nun's mouth set in a sneer and she turned her back to Sister María Inés. Facing the wall, she said: 'All these years I served you with love and obedience. But what you did was horrible. May God have mercy on you.'

Sister María Inés checked her anger. 'You may rest another day. Then I expect you in the chapel.'

In the days that followed Sister María Inés avoided the nuns. She led the daily prayers in the chapel but did not speak to them unless it was to give them instructions for their duties. She did not greet them when she came across them or acknowledge their presence even with a glance. In the refectory, she ate quickly and then returned to her room, where she spent most of her time, caring for the child and reading the books she fetched from the library. A few times she was seen in the shed working on the Ford. She began to mistrust everyone and became suspicious of the slightest sound: the rats in the corners of the room, the owls in the roof, the footsteps outside her door, the clanking of the pans in the kitchen. It was not an unreasonable fear. Sister Beatriz had told her that Sister Ana had been to the city and spoken to the Bishop.

At least Sister Beatriz was still her ally and helped her with the child, despite being as shocked by her actions as the other nuns. Sister Beatriz knocked on her door, in fact, more often than ever, making Sister María Inés suspect that it was because she no longer trusted her with the child. To prove the young woman wrong, Sister María Inés was even more attentive to him. She still allowed Sister Beatriz to prepare his milk but mostly fed him herself. Having long forgotten the songs of her childhood, which in itself had become an implausible memory at her age, she had to invent her own lullabies and nursery rhymes for the child. She sang them only if she was certain that there was no one within earshot, not so much because she knew that she was contradicting herself when she had reprimanded Sister Teresa for her singing (she no longer cared whether or not the sisters respected her decisions so long as they obeyed them), but because she was aware of the limitations of her own voice. In one of the abandoned buildings of the convent, she found, under thick cobwebs, the sewing machine a seamstress had used to make the habits of the new arrivals in the former days of glory, when the convent was home to tens of nuns. Sister María Inés asked Sister Beatriz to help her carry it to her room and fix it so that she could sew clothes for the child, which she then dyed in bright colours and embroidered with figures of cherubs, birds and flowers in gold.

One day, taking a break from her sewing, she wrapped the child in a blanket and went for a walk. She came across nobody on her way out. Outside the convent she stood on the steps and tried to recall the day they had found the child a few weeks earlier. It had still been warm then, while now, even though it was a bright day, she was shivering inside her habit. She carefully climbed down the slippery steps; there was still some morning dew on the stone. There was no wind at all, the pine trees did not move and the only sounds that she could hear were the chirping of the birds and her hobnailed boots on the stones. She followed the road for some time before entering the wood at a place where the tree growth was not dense, and walked sure-footed on the rough ground carpeted with pine needles and twigs that snapped pleasantly under her feet. Very few rays of sun passed through the canopy of the trees. She stopped and listened. When she had first joined the convent, silence used to make her ill at ease, for she had grown up in a house dominated by the din of human voices, the music from the Edison phonograph and the songs of caged birds, but over time she had come to terms with silence.

She knew her way around the woods and walked deeper in, not forgetting that soon it would be time for the midday prayer – she could return quickly if she had to. The child in her arms was awake. She now knew that she was sincere when she had promised to defend him with her life: she had kept her word. There was little doubt in her mind that the attack by the dog had been a deliberate test of her dedication. She said softly: '*Examine me, O Lord, and prove me; try my reins and my heart.*' She was a mother at last even if she had not given birth herself – only God could make such a miracle.

She thought she heard something – something that sounded out of place. She spent a lot of time in the woods and her ears were able to pick out the slightest sound that did not belong to nature. She stopped and listened but it was gone. She took a few cautious steps and there the sound was again. It would have been imperceptible to anyone else, but Sister María Inés had no doubt that it was the sound of footsteps on the dry needles: someone or something was following her. After so much talk about the Devil, his image flashed through her mind and she shuddered: the cloven hooves, the twisted horns, the bat-like wings. She squeezed the child in her arms and began a short prayer. When she came to a very old tree, she hid behind its trunk and waited, cradling the child in her arms to keep him silent.

Her stalker was coming. He was taking a few slow steps, then stopping, then moving cautiously again. Sister María Inés continued to pray silently: *Satanam aliosque spiritus malignos, qui ad perditionem animarum pervagantur in mundo . . .* The footsteps came closer. Whoever it was, he was now only a few trees away. Sister María Inés looked at the child. He was falling asleep from her rocking. A moment later a shadow went past only a few feet away. The Mother Superior studied it from behind and then asked in a stern voice: 'What exactly are you doing here?'

Sister Beatriz let out a shriek and turned round. 'You gave me the fright of my life, Reverend Mother. I thought perhaps you wanted company.'

The child had fallen asleep, and the Mother Superior lowered her voice. 'Stop following me around,' she said. 'Are you against me too, Beatriz?'

'No, I am with you, Mother.'

'Do you want them to take the child and put him away in an orphanage?'

'No, Mother.'

'Because no one will take this child away. God brought him to me for a reason.'

The nun stood obediently, not daring to say anything. The Mother Superior slowly calmed down. She asked: 'Don't you believe in miracles, Beatriz? No matter how rare, they still happen. You see . . .'

But she stopped because she felt that what she wanted to say about God and Divine Providence was too important to be said out there in the woods. She thought: 'Why is it that only I can see the truth?' Perhaps it was because she was the only one in the convent who truly believed in God. All of them of course obeyed the rules of the Order and did good acts, but true faith was something altogether different. If only she could explain it to the young woman . . .

They started to head back to the convent, as it was almost time for prayers. They went through the woods, their feet sinking into the thick carpet of pine needles. The fear was gone now and Sister María Inés was thinking about her miraculous motherhood again. With every step some form of life stirred round her –

in the trees, in the air, under the earth. She felt love not just for the child in her arms but also for the young woman who followed behind her. It was good to have company. She promised to be good to Beatriz from then on. The air smelled of pine, and she felt her boots getting wet from the dew that had not dried under the shade of the trees. They had almost reached the edge of the woods when she woke up from her ecstasy and recognised, with a ripple of unease, the sound of the Bishop's car coming fast up the road.

The Bishop shut the car door and took off his leather helmet. Powdered with dust, his face had the pallor of a dead man. Travelling was the least favourite part of his duties but it was necessary. Moreover, his suffering after an hour at the wheel was not a bad way of reminding himself that in the eyes of God he was not as important as his high rank led people to believe. He shook his coat and disappeared in a cloud of dust that made him cough. '*In wisdom hast Thou made them all,*' he murmured. 'But there was no need for so much dust.'

He took a bottle of eau de cologne out of his pocket, sprinkled a little on his handkerchief and cleaned his face until it recovered its splendour and the tenacity of a Roman emperor. When the Mother Superior came forward to kiss his ring, Bishop Estrada spoke to her as if she had asked him a question: 'I am afraid I cannot stay the night. I have lots of work back at the see.'

'We are so pleased to see you, Your Excellency,' the Mother Superior said.

'It is nice to see you again, Sister. I wish I did not have to come, though. Oh, I only mean *today*. You know how much I enjoy visiting you. I wish this were one of our blessed Sundays. Alas, it is not a very happy occasion.'

'Since you are here, Your Excellency, you might be so kind as to say Mass this evening.'

The Bishop hesitated for a moment, but then said: 'By all means, Sister. I always have time for that.'

The nuns came to kiss his ring too, and he blessed them, staring silently at each woman who bowed in front of him. Even

127

Sister Carlota had come out of her room, for the first time since the poisoning of the dogs. After the Bishop had blessed all the nuns, he turned to the Mother Superior again and spoke to her in a low voice. 'Let me first of all say how much I dislike these things. A complaint was made about you and I am obliged to investigate because I consider this place to be under my personal care. Besides, we would not want this matter to reach ears that stand higher from the ground than ours.'

The Mother Superior bowed. 'We are grateful for your discretion, Your Excellency.'

'I do not consider it a serious matter. But admittedly, it is unusual,' the Bishop said. They were still standing at the entrance to the convent, where his diplomat's instinct told him to wait a moment longer. He asked in a louder voice that had lost its earlier formality: 'And how are you, Sister?'

'The Blessed Virgin is looking after us, Your Excellency.'

'Is she also looking after the car?'

'Yes, Your Excellency. Only little things now and then, but they are easily fixed.'

'I wish I could have made you a better gift, Sister.'

'Oh no, it has made a great difference, Your Excellency. You have been very generous to us as it is.'

Now the two of them entered the convent, followed by the nuns. The Mother Superior turned towards the guesthouse but the Bishop stopped her. 'No, Sister. Thank you. Let us go straight to your office.'

'You do not need to rest at all, Your Excellency?'

'Later – if there is time left. I would rather get this over with.'

They turned back and took the stairs to the Mother Superior's room. Beside the bed, just beyond the reach of the daylight coming through the narrow windows, was the cradle where the child lay sleeping. The Mother Superior followed the Bishop inside and the other nuns squeezed in behind them. Without hurrying, the Bishop took off his coat, hung it on the wall and made to go towards the cradle. The Mother Superior stopped him with a respectful reminder: 'Your *shoes*, Your Excellency. The poor thing has just gone to sleep.'

Bishop Estrada looked at his feet and his eyebrows arched. Trying to make as little noise as possible on the wooden floor, he approached the cradle. 'So this is your latest recruit,' he whispered, making the sign of the Cross over the child. 'The arrival of a new life is always a happy occasion, no matter the circumstances.'

'I believe so too, Your Excellency,' the Mother Superior said.

The other nuns received his words with silence. The Bishop was quick to understand that it was not what they had expected from him. He added with a sigh: 'Whoever abandoned this child committed a grave sin. And now we are left to deal with the consequences.' The windows were closed to keep the room warm for the child and the air smelled of regurgitated milk. The Bishop recognised the smell from his January visits to the city orphanage, where he gave the children presents, dressed in a gold-threaded robe and with his face blackened by charcoal to look like Balthasar, the magus from the East. He looked at the child again and thought of the Old Testament story of Solomon and the baby with two mothers. Then he turned to the nuns and said that he would like to speak to all of them.

'Please wait outside to be called in one at a time.'

'Do you wish me to be present at the interviews, Your Excellency?' the Mother Superior asked.

No, he did not because he should not be seen to favour her over the other nuns. Sister María Inés understood. 'Then allow me to take the child to another room,' she said.

'Find somewhere quiet for him.'

When the Bishop was left alone, he experienced the familiar discomfort that had been plaguing him recently every time he visited the convent. Once he used to like to sit in this room with the Mother Superior and discuss the affairs of the convent. He liked the arched windows that seemed to let in the same amount of light no matter how bright the day was, the modesty of the furniture, the smell of incense, the sound of his feet on the wooden floor, the cool fortress walls which had withstood the repeated attacks of Hayreddin Barbarossa and his corsairs. But today the room seemed to him stifling and steeped in grief.

For some time now he had been dreading his visits to the convent despite the peaceful countryside, the beautiful garden, the long lunch under the vine in the company of the sisters who adored him. He wished, in fact, to appoint another confessor to them, a decision he was in no doubt was the right one, even though he had not told the Mother Superior or anyone else yet and did not intend to until he had found the appropriate person to replace him.

He went to the door and asked to see first the nun who had found the baby on the steps of the convent. Sister Lucía entered the room. Bishop Estrada said in a calm voice: 'Do not be afraid. I am not here to accuse anyone. I only want to know the facts.' He was aware that his manner and his long black cassock with the purple sash made people stand in awe of him. If sometimes he did nothing to put them at ease, he liked to think that he did it not out of vanity but because he considered it necessary to inspire his flock with obedience. On this occasion, however, it was obvious to him that such an approach would hinder his investigation and he smiled. 'You ought to be proud of what you did, Sister,' he said. 'You saved a human life. Tell me about it.' As soon as the nun began to speak, he stopped her by raising his hand. 'Start from the moment you opened your eyes that morning,' he said. Sister Lucía tried to remember what she had done that fateful day, from the time she had got out of bed for dawn prayer until she had walked out of the convent to go to the car.

'The car you so kindly gave us, Your Excellency,' she said.

The Bishop asked: 'Where do you keep it?'

'In the donkey's shed behind the chapel. One has to go out of the convent to get there.'

'Isn't Sister Beatriz responsible for buying the provisions in the city?'

'The Reverend Mother had been sending me in her place, Your Excellency.'

She said that until she had left the convent she had heard nothing suspicious, noticed nothing strange and had carried out her tasks as usual. Then she described how she had seen the suitcase at the bottom of the steps, looked through the holes cut in it and what she had seen inside. 'It was unbelievable. At first I thought it was a doll.'

Bishop Estrada asked where the suitcase was.

'It's in the Reverend Mother's wardrobe, Your Excellency.'

'Bring it to me, please.'

He examined the old suitcase inside and out but it gave him no clues to the mystery and he asked the nun to put it back. When he had no more questions to ask her, he thanked her for her help and told her to send in the next nun. He saw Sister Teresa briefly and then Sister Carlota, who stayed with him for some time telling him about the poisoning of the dogs and insisting that the Mother Superior was possessed. Feeling sorry for her grief, the Bishop did not contradict her. When she came out of the room leaning on his arm, she raised her head, dried her eyes and pointed at the Mother Superior. 'It's her fault,' she said. 'God help us.' Bishop Estrada smiled at the Mother Superior with understanding and beckoned to Sister Beatriz.

'I understand you no longer drive the car,' the Bishop said when they were alone in the room.

'I will start again soon. I had asked to be excused, Your Excellency.'

He asked her to sit and stared at her while his fingers played with his ring. The room continued to depress him. The matter with the child did not seem to him to be serious and he regretted having come. He could have sent someone else. Then he remembered that he had promised Sister Ana. He asked: 'What is your opinion of the Mother Superior?'

'She is very kind. I think she is right to want to keep the orphan. It is the Christian thing to do.'

'Are you helping her with him?'

'Only a little. When she has to be elsewhere. I am glad to. She is very competent. Do you know that she used to be a nurse?'

'Yes. What do you think I should do?'

'The baby does no one any harm, Your Excellency.'

'But the Mother Superior committed a terrible act because of him.'

'The dogs? Only after one almost killed her. You should have seen it.'

'Nevertheless, Sister Carlota is very distressed.'

The young nun did not disagree. 'It was a cruel thing killing them, yes. But if you had seen how that dog attacked the baby you would understand.'

'I am told you were the only one who tried to help her when she was in danger.'

'Ah that. If only I was brave enough.'

'Apparently you were. It was the others who held you back.'

'The poor child would have been harmed – but the Reverend Mother saved him.'

After a few more questions Bishop Estrada sent her away with a sad smile and a few words that sounded like a farewell: 'Look after yourself. And come to see me if there is anything that I can do for you.' Sister Beatriz raised her head and looked straight at him for the first time during their discussion. The Bishop realised that he had almost given away his secret desire to resign from his responsibility to the nuns and rushed to add: 'I will see you all on Sunday, as usual.'

The nun left the room with a silent bow. He watched her go, regretting his comment. It was almost midday and the rising temperature was causing him to sweat under his heavy cassock. He opened a window, leaned out and took a deep breath, looking at his car parked beside the steps to the convent and covered with dust. The thought of the trip back to the city filled him with dismay. He was in good condition for a man of his age but his problem was more of the mind. Lately he had been toying with the idea of pushing for the post of apostolic nuncio in a quiet mission abroad. It would not be impossible. After all, he had studied diplomacy and had some powerful friends in the Vatican. Wanting to rest a little, he lay on the narrow bed in the corner of the room but immediately winced at the hardness of the mattress. He thought: 'O God, anything, anywhere but here . . . Why did I come? . . . Forgive me . . .' There was a knock on the door and before he could answer Sister Ana entered with a packet.

'Excuse me, Your Excellency,' she said. 'I had no idea you were resting. I will come back a little later.'

The Bishop waved her in and rose slowly. 'Never mind, Sister. There is work to be done. Please come in.' Then he saw the packet and his mouth puckered. 'Another present? Now, Sister, I am afraid I cannot accept any more presents from you.'

'No, Your Excellency. This is in connection with the investigation. It is very important.'

Bishop Estrada sat at the desk and watched the nun unfold the brown paper with delicate movements. She took out the soiled bed sheet, spread it over the desk as if it were a tablecloth and took a step back. The Bishop looked at the large bloodstain and turned to the nun. Her face showed no trace of clemency. 'And what is this, Sister?' he asked.

'Indisputable evidence of Devil worship, Your Excellency – here in our convent.'

She told him where she had discovered it and how she had searched for other evidence of sorcery, which she had finally found in one of the rooms of the old school for novices: traces of blood on the newly mopped floor. She believed that everything was connected with the arrival of the child. She added: 'Even before I came across these signs of witchcraft I had been against the Mother Superior's intention of keeping the orphan. I tried to warn the sisters but they didn't listen. I admit that I haven't confronted the Mother Superior with what I have found because I fear for my life. But after the poisoning of the dogs I had to act and so I came to see you.'

The Bishop leaned over the cloth and said: 'We cannot be certain how long this thing has been buried. The stain could be very old.'

'Perhaps, Your Excellency. But whoever mopped the floor in the abandoned building had done it very recently.'

'And what does the child have to do with all this?' the Bishop asked. Then, remembering their conversation in his office, he answered his own question: 'Oh yes, the spawn of Satan. I forgot.'

'We need an exorcist, Your Excellency.'

'Or Sherlock Holmes' the Bishop said with a well-meaning smile.

He asked the nun to show him where she had found the bed sheet. When they came out of the room, he told the Mother Superior to wait for him and followed Sister Ana. They went to a corner of the convent where the nun pointed to the exact place the dog had dug out the bed sheet. Then he asked her to show him the room where she had found the signs of the satanic ceremony and they crossed the courtyard and entered the school for novices. The wind blowing in through the broken windows had deposited small heaps of earth where grey plants without flowers grew in the gloom with the help of the damp. Bishop Estrada followed the nun up the creaking staircase. The corner where Sister Ana had come across the traces of blood appeared no different from the rest of the room. Since her discovery, dust had covered the floor again and erased every sign of the blood and the mopping. She knelt and brushed the dust with her hands in vain. She said: 'It was here, Your Excellency. If you look closely between the boards . . . You see?'

The Bishop bent down but saw nothing. 'Yes, perhaps,' he said and stood up again.

'Maybe there is something elsewhere – in one of the other rooms. I searched them already but perhaps you could be more thorough.'

Bishop Estrada had seen that exasperation many times, that determined stony face, that relentless struggle against the rest of the world: a lost soul. He turned away and looked at the broken furniture and the plaster that was peeling away from the damp walls. 'Let us go now, Sister,' he said. 'I have seen enough. It is a long time since God was last in this place.'

The nun stood up and cleaned her hands.

'Could it not be one of the dogs, Sister?' the Bishop asked.

'A *dog*, Your Excellency? In here?'

'Yes. One of the late lamented dogs. They were free to go anywhere in the convent.'

'Yes, Your Excellency. But the mopped floor, the—'

'Was it really mopped? No person in their right mind would come in here.'

'There is blood on the sheet, too.'

'It could have been lying buried for years. Besides, what does it prove? Do you have any idea whose blood it is? Has there been a crime?'

'I believe it was a ritual, Your Excellency.' And the woman added with fear: 'A dog was sacrificed.'

'Have you asked Sister Carlota if any of the dogs had gone missing? She will tell you – unless she is behind all this. But this is very unlikely, don't you think? She loved those dogs like her own family.'

'I am not accusing Carlota. The poor woman is innocent, of course. But there has to be an explanation.'

'Perhaps you were a little too eager to draw your conclusions,' the Bishop said. He patted her on the arm to temper his criticism and spoke in a tone that implied his last word on the matter: 'Demons or not, it was right to let me know about the child. I thank you. Now I have to make up my mind what to do about him.'

He could tell that she was very disappointed. They walked with care on the unstable floorboards, keeping well clear of the holes through which they could see the floor below, and came out of the derelict building. The other nuns had gathered in the courtyard to wait for them. Bishop Estrada said nothing about the search. He thanked the sisters for their help and honesty, told Sister María Inés that it would take him a few days to deliberate on the matter of the child and drove off while it was still day.

He could see the tiled roofs of the city when he realised that, confused by so many speculations, by the bitter venom of so many accusations and by his own desperation to get away, he had in fact forgotten that he had promised the Mother Superior to say Mass in the convent that evening.

First to leave were the storks that had been born in the convent that summer, but Sister Beatriz did not realise the birds were leaving until, some days later, the older birds also began to join the flocks that were gathering in the salt-water marshes near the sea for the journey to Africa. They were taking off from the rooftops throughout the day, from early in the morning, when the nuns crossed the courtyard to go to the chapel, until dusk, each pair leaving together, heading south in a straight path. By the end of the week all the nests were empty, several days earlier than in any of the previous years. The nuns did not give it any more thought until Sunday morning, when the Bishop was late for Mass. Then they began to suspect that the departure of the birds had been a bad omen and gathered on the steps outside the convent to wait, afraid that something might have happened to him. Only the Mother Superior remained in her room.

It was almost noon when they saw a man on a mule coming up the road. He was urging the animal on but was obviously a bad rider and the mule continued to walk at a leisurely pace. When he came closer, the nuns saw that he was a young priest in a cordovan hat and a buttoned-up cassock, but the strangest thing about him was the stick with a carrot tied to its end that he held in front of the mule's head. He stopped in front of the steps, got down from the mule and straightened his cassock in a self-conscious manner under the stares of the women. After he had rewarded the mule with the carrot, he took his hat off to the nuns and said: 'His Excellency sends his apologies. It wasn't possible for him to come.'

His name was Father Mateo and the nuns took an instant dislike to him despite his modesty. He had neither the Bishop's importance of manner, which inspired respect and trust, nor his good looks and elegance. They looked at his pitted face, his long nose and big ears, which were exaggerated by his hair being cropped very short, and dismissed his humility not as a virtuous choice but as the inevitable fate of any ugly man. Without welcoming him, they asked after the Bishop and he reassured them several times in his timid voice that he was in good health, that as far as he knew his car had not broken down, that he had no bad feeling towards them but, on the contrary, loved them and missed them as always. Then he said that His Excellency had entrusted him with a letter addressed to the Mother Superior, whom his eyes searched for among the nuns. Sister Beatriz told him to wait and went to fetch her. When Sister María Inés appeared at the door of the convent, she was no more friendly towards him than the nuns. 'You are not who you should be, Father,' she said.

'His Excellency has sent me on his behalf, Reverend Mother.'

'But I assume that he did not tell you to be late.'

The young man had the easy blush of a Virgo. 'The trip took longer than I expected,' he said. 'I couldn't get the animal to go any faster. When I remembered the trick with the carrot it was already late.' He searched his pockets and with a ceremonial gesture handed the Mother Superior an envelope bearing the Bishop's coat of arms. 'His Excellency asked me to convey his personal regards.'

Sister María Inés received the letter without a comment. She had waited for it all week, had dreamed about it while she slept, had thought about it with dread every time she led the prayers in the chapel. Keeping her calm, she tore open the envelope and read the letter in silence. The nuns observed her.

When she finished she pursed her lips and stood for a moment deep in thought. 'I see,' she said.

'Is it about the child?' Sister Beatriz asked.

Instead of an answer the Mother Superior gave the nuns a quick paraphrase of the letter: 'His Excellency regrets having to surrender his post of confessor to our convent with immediate effect. His demanding schedule does not allow him . . . et cetera. He believes the Reverend Father here will prove a more than worthy successor . . . and he is most grateful to us for our kindness and hospitality.'

It was unexpected because the Bishop had always seemed to enjoy their company. Looking at the young priest of whose abilities they already had a low opinion, the nuns wondered why His Excellency had made this decision that broke their hearts, and they concluded that it had something to do with the child. Sister Ana said: 'We demand to read the letter ourselves.'

The Mother Superior looked at her with scorn. 'I am not obliged to show it to you,' she said, but handed it to her.

At the bottom of the page, below the typed text, a few words had been added in Bishop Estrada's own hand. Sister Ana read them out: 'As regards the matter of the orphan, I intend to inform you of my decision in due course. In the interim, I am certain you will continue to care for him with the commendable kindness you have shown him so far.'

She gave back the letter and left the gathering with an icy expression. When the bell rang a little while later, she overcame her frustration and joined the sisters in the chapel, where Father Mateo prepared to say Sunday Mass. It was the first time that he had ever stood in front of a congregation alone, and his fright was obvious in his uncertain voice, his shaking hand, the mistakes that made the Mother Superior sigh with disapproval.

He had been ordained only a month earlier and Bishop Estrada believed that he was a good choice for priest and confessor to the nuns despite his inexperience, or, rather, because of it: a discreet first post before he moved him on to a larger congregation that right now would be too testing for his abilities. Father Mateo had accepted his post without objections. His duties were to say Mass and listen to confessions at the convent every Sunday and at important religious celebrations. Bishop Estrada had reassured him that he would have no problems. He had said: 'The nuns are very devout. But if you hear anything out of the ordinary I remind you of the Seal of the Confessional.'

'Of course, Your Excellency,' the young man said, astonished. 'I am well aware of that.'

The Bishop fixed him with a fierce glance. 'Good. Or else I will not hesitate to excommunicate you.'

He put his hand in his pocket and gave the young man a few banknotes from his wallet, less out of generosity than a wish to lighten the mood of the meeting, which had turned oppressive after his warning. 'Here, Father. Buy yourself a mule that won't die this year,' he said and sent him away with a blessing and a final piece of advice: 'Always do your duty and come straight back. Do not spend the night in the convent even if you have to ride in the dark.'

Sister María Inés came to Mass with the child in her arms. Father Mateo was not surprised. The Bishop had talked to him about the matter that was a headache to him. When the priest ended the service and walked towards the sacristy to take off his vestments, relieved that his torment had ended, the Mother Superior hurried up to him. 'One moment, Father,' she said. 'You also have to baptise the child.'

The priest was unprepared for her request. He had received no advice from the Bishop about that. 'I don't think it's possible, Mother.'

'It is more than a month since he was born. He should have been baptised already.'

'Yes, but I will have to ask His Excellency.'

'Are you denying this child the sacrament of baptism?'

'No, no, what I mean is . . .' The priest looked at the nuns pleadingly, but they were silent.

'Delaying the baptism may put his salvation in danger, Father,' Sister María Inés said. 'What if something were to happen to him?'

'Yes, of course. However—'

'You have no right to deny it, Father.'

'No, no, of course not, Mother. I'm not denying anything. I'm only thinking that if we waited a few days . . . Next Sunday perhaps? By then I will have had the chance to speak to His Excellency.'

'No, Father. You have to do it today. You are responsible if anything happens to this unbaptised child.'

Father Mateo nodded. 'Very well.'

It was already afternoon, with a beautiful autumnal sunlight coming through the small windows of the chapel, when Sister María Inés unwrapped the blanket. The child was dressed in a white christening gown. She had sewn it herself and decorated it with satin cherubs and metal sequins taken from one of her old dresses, which she kept in a cedar chest scattered with rosemary and mint leaves to repel the moths. She had been thinking of this moment ever since she had made the decision to keep the child, but the need to baptise him had become even more urgent after the attack of the dog made her fear that something might happen to him and he would be denied salvation.

'Where is the baptismal font?' the priest asked.

There had been no need for one in a convent. The Mother Superior called Sister Beatriz and told her: 'Fetch the baking tray from the kitchen.'

The priest pouted but said nothing. 'The godparents?' he asked.

'Only one,' the Mother Superior said. 'Sister Beatriz.'

The nun returned with the tray from the kitchen and took the child in her arms without objection.

'His name?'

'Renato,' Sister María Inés said. 'The one who was born again.'

The priest poured holy water onto the child's head: '*Renato ego te baptizo in nomine Patris et Filii et Spiritus Sancti.*'

Sister Ana had left as they started, convinced that the baptism was another part of the Mother Superior's evil plans. The other nuns stayed. When the ceremony ended, Sister Beatriz returned the child to the Mother Superior, who asked Father Mateo to stay for lunch. Remembering the Bishop's advice, the priest begged to be excused. He took off his liturgical vestments and put them away, asked for a carrot to set the mule in motion and took the road back to the city.

After lunch Sister Beatriz came to the Mother Superior's room to thank her for making her the child's godmother. But she was worried about the child's fate. 'Do you think we're going to hear from His Excellency soon, Mother?'

'I hope so.'

'I'm afraid of this delay. He might decide against keeping him. Maybe he is waiting for a reply from the orphanage.'

'Who knows?' the Mother Superior said. 'I used to think he was a wise man.'

'The sisters all agree that he listened very carefully to them.'

'I think he ought to have listened to what I had to say too. But at least he does not seem to be swayed by Sister Ana's lies.'

They sat looking at the child dressed in the white gown. Sister Beatriz said: 'I don't think His Excellency likes us very much. Otherwise he wouldn't have abandoned us.'

'He likes us enough,' the Mother Superior said. 'He was our confessor, not our parent.' In truth, she was as worried as the young nun. 'Renato has no place in an orphanage. I promise you that, as I promise God.'

She could not tell when the child had become hers, *really* hers, but when she had stood beside the priest and Sister Beatriz at the altar that day for the christening, she had believed beyond a shadow of a doubt that she had given birth to the child herself. She believed it with absolute conviction despite its implausibility, despite the fact that no one else in the world seemed to believe it, and no argument to the contrary could make her change her mind. She knew, of course, that she had not slept with anyone in order to conceive, nor had she given birth after nine months of pregnancy; the child was God's miraculous reward for her sincere remorse during all those years. She fed him when he needed to be fed; she kept him warm when he was cold; she had saved him when he had been in mortal danger and would continue to do so for as long as she was alive. She now tucked him up in his cradle and said with her back to Sister Beatriz: 'You will look after Renato tomorrow. I have to go to the city.'

The city had been built in Roman times on the banks of a river that poured into the ocean more than a hundred miles away, across a marshy estuary where the storks gathered every autumn to travel to Africa. Minarets and other ruins of an empire now lost in the annals of history rose above the cobbled squares, the old palaces, the exquisite gardens looked after by the worthy descendants of Babylonian gardeners whose secrets they had sworn to reveal only to their successors. The mosque that dated back to the thirteenth century also survived but had long been converted into a cathedral with giant arches, columns of jasper and marble, a honeycombed dome with blue tiles and a courtyard planted with orange trees. The only truly living memory of the time of the Moors was the scented steam coming out of the old baths, which had been shut down after the Christians had recaptured the city but had later reopened with the consent of the Church.

When the wind began to blow, the narrow streets still echoed with the immortal ramblings of the ancient philosophers who had tried to make sense of the world, the heartbreaking cries of those who had been burned alive in cruel autos-da-fé and the maddening gypsy music of the present day. The winters rarely had frosts but it still rained a great deal, a rain mixed with the soot of the fireplaces that burned coal from the Sierra Morena. In the summer there were frequent droughts of extreme heat which baked the earth and made the cobbles smoulder. In the hot air rising from the ground, the mirage of the cathedral could then be seen for miles. Dressed in his cassock and zucchetto, the Bishop would take shelter from the insanity of the summer heat at the altar and would exorcise his thirst with cupfuls of holy water mixed with rose petals and ice.

It was a long time since Sister María Inés had been to the city. She only drove there twice a year, once to attend the diocesan council and a second time to take the train to the capital for her annual visit to the Superioress General. The rest of the time she was happy to shun the world and to send Sister Beatriz for the convent supplies.

Today the sky was clear and she had folded back the roof of the Ford, impervious to the cold mountain wind that followed her on her journey until she reached the bottom of the valley where the city lay. The trip had taken her more than two hours, much longer than she had expected, because she had to stop several times and top up the radiator with water. When she reached the first houses of the city, she crossed herself with a sigh of relief. She left the car at a garage to have its radiator fixed and walked across the city towards the column with the statue of Archangel Raphael, the city's guardian.

Not far from there was the Bishop's Palace, sheltered from the clamour of the streets behind a row of poplars which had grown over the years into a wall of dense foliage. As soon as Sister María Inés crossed the threshold of the palace, the cries of vendors, the noise of cars, the sound of horses' hooves on the cobbles died away. She walked through an arched passage to the courtyard, where the only sound was the murmur of running water in a small fountain, and climbed the stairs to the waiting room, where a young deacon sat writing at a desk. He asked her if she had an appointment.

'No. But I do not mind waiting.'

'It might take a long time,' the deacon said frostily.

'I do not mind,' Sister María Inés said. 'I have been waiting all my life.'

The man made a face and pretended to look through the big diary spread open in front of him. Finally he left his desk without hurry, opened the door to the Bishop's office just enough to slip through and returned a moment later with the same sullen expression. He said: 'His Excellency will see you now.'

The Bishop was in a better mood than his secretary. He showed the Mother Superior to a gilded sofa and made a light-hearted comment: 'I am afraid the furniture in this room is too ornate to be comfortable.' He sat in an armchair and added with more humour: 'I suspect it was purposely made that way to keep visits brief – but please feel free to stay as long as you like.'

After a silence that seemed to last for a long time, he asked: 'What is your impression of Father Mateo?'

'We did not expect him.'

'Are you not happy with him?'

Sister María Inés said that they were.

'I know that he is not experienced, but he is very committed,' Bishop Estrada said. 'Please have patience with him. It is very difficult to find someone to fill a post that is so far away from everywhere.'

'We like to believe we are perhaps a little closer to God, Your Excellency.'

'Quite,' the Bishop said. 'But to get to heaven and back every Sunday the poor Father has to sit on a mule for ten hours.'

The Mother Superior did not persist. 'He is very welcome. And I will personally do everything I can to assist him.'

The Bishop sat in contemplation of the vast room. After a while he said: 'He also told me about the baptism.'

'I hope Your Excellency does not think it was improper of me to have asked him.'

The Bishop smiled. 'You did not *ask* him, Sister. He says you *forced* him to do it. Anyway, I do not think it was wrong at all.'

'I wish it had been you who performed the sacrament. But I missed the chance to ask you on your last visit.'

Bishop Estrada remembered how he had left the convent without having said Mass as he had promised. He said: 'I would have been honoured. But I had to leave. It was one of those occasions when duty forces me to make a trip I do not like.'

Sister María Inés took a deep breath and said: 'I came to see you because we did not have the opportunity to speak in private last time.'

'I already know where you stand on the matter, Sister. But I am glad that you came. I do not want you to think I ignored you or that I am being unfair in any way.'

'I never thought that of you, Your Excellency.'

'Good,' Bishop Estrada said and got up from his seat. He stood at the window, whose heavy drapes were tied back; only a pair of muslin curtains hung across the glass. He parted them with a finger and observed the tall column with the statue of the Archangel in the square. 'Your request is highly unusual,' he said. 'Highly unusual.'

'It would be no more than doing my Christian duty.'

'Would it? I am not convinced. As you know, there is an orphanage in the city.'

'In an institution like that . . . Of course, it is a great blessing that it exists. I know your great commitment to it. But with so many children it is inevitable that Renato would not get the attention he would be receiving in the convent.'

'It seems to me that you are the only one who wants him there.'

'I believe Sister Beatriz also agrees with me, Your Excellency. She has a great affection for him.'

The Bishop nodded without enthusiasm. 'Oh yes, Sister Beatriz.'

'I am prepared to do anything for the child. I will care for him until he is at least old enough to go to school.'

'You did not have to poison the dogs, Sister.'

'I do not regret it. They were likely to harm him. I feel sorry for Sister Carlota, of course.'

The Bishop did not really care about the dogs. He said: 'The child has to be properly registered. There is always the chance, no matter how remote, that the real mother will come forward.'

'Oh, there is no mother, Your Excellency.'

'I beg your pardon?'

Sister María Inés hesitated whether to tell the Bishop that the coming of the child was a miracle. In the end she decided against it and said simply: 'I mean that a mother who abandons her child does not deserve to be called a mother.'

'Although legally she still is,' the Bishop said. 'And there is also the mystery of the bloodied sheet.'

Then he told her, in a frank and serious voice, about the bed sheet that Sister Ana had showed him and their search round the convent for more evidence of the presence of evil. Sister María Inés showed no emotion when the Bishop said that the other woman suspected her of being under the influence of Satan. He added: 'I do not need to tell you, of course, that I do not believe one iota of what she says about you.' Nevertheless, the accusations filled him with dismay because they could only be the creations of a disturbed mind. 'I want to hear your opinion,' he concluded.

'I have not seen that bed sheet,' Sister María Inés said. 'But it is undoubtedly a fabricated piece of evidence.'

The Bishop looked at her keenly. 'You think so too?'

'It only takes a splash of paint.'

'I know. But it has to be said that Sister Ana seems genuinely terrified about it.'

'I hope you do not think it more likely that I am possessed, Your Excellency.'

'No, Sister. I simply believe that the sheet could have been there for a number of years. The fact that it was buried is odd, of course, but I do not believe it has anything to do with you or the child.'

The door opened and the deacon came gliding in. Bishop Estrada said: 'Yes, I am coming, Ignacio. Thank you.' The young man went away and the Bishop made a gesture of helplessness. 'A busy schedule,' he said. 'Anyhow, Sister, I admire your dedication to that poor child. My first instinct is to let you keep him.'

Sister María Inés stood up from the sofa and bowed to kiss his ring. 'Thank you, Your Excellency. You will not regret it.'

The Bishop withdrew his hand. 'Do not thank me yet. I have not decided. I must think very carefully about this.' He sighed. 'It is harder than squaring the circle. Sister Ana is only one variable in the equation. What about the other sisters? They do not agree with you either.'

'It is only because of Sister Ana. If Your Excellency arranged it so that she moved somewhere else I am confident I can make them see sense.'

They left it at that. Sister María Inés bowed again and this time Bishop Estrada allowed her to kiss his ring with the silent understanding that he was very likely to deliberate in her favour. She left his office calmer than when she had arrived and made her way across the palace without a hurry. Reluctant to leave that paradise and face the madness of the city, which after so many years of solitude terrified her, she sat on a bench in the courtyard and immersed herself in the serene beauty of the garden. There was nobody about. Attracted by the trickling fountain, a pair of birds splashed in the water. More birds sat on the rim of the fountain, and she picked up the rosary looped round her belt and began: '*In nomine Patris et Filii et Spiritus Sancti* . . .' She had not finished when the deacon came up to her and asked her if she wanted anything else. Sensing that she was unwelcome, she finished her prayer quickly and went away.

At the garage the car was not yet ready and she looked for a place to have lunch. When she came back, the garage was shut. She had forgotten it was the time of the siesta – she never slept in the afternoons herself. She went for a walk across the sleeping city until it was time for the garage to reopen, gazing with admiration at the windows on either side of the narrow streets with their ornate iron grilles and pots of roses and jasmine.

The orphanage of San Rafael the Healer stood on the edge of the city and had been built with the support of Bishop Estrada, who had given the project, soon after his consecration, priority over the erection of churches across the diocese. He donated the land on behalf of the Church, paid for the furnishing of the wards, advertised it in every parish and established an annual bazaar towards its upkeep. At the time his decision had caused a scandal among the most pious members of the local community, who had interpreted his generous support for the orphans as an encouragement for men and women to sin. But the Vatican had stood behind him and a letter of support from Pope Pius XI had been read in every church of the diocese to placate the firebrands, though many of them doubted even the authenticity of the stamp with the papal emblem in red ink. Several years had passed since then and now everyone acknowledged Bishop Estrada's charity and foresight, but the money raised at the annual bazaar was not enough. The orphanage suffered from a perpetual lack of funds which worsened as a result of the steady increase in the number of orphans.

It was the first time that Sister María Inés had visited the orphanage and she was struck by the similarity between the suitcase that had been left on the steps of her convent and the night depository for babies: on the wall next to the gated entrance, a few feet above the ground, was a small perforated cupboard lined with wool blankets where during the night one could leave a baby, unseen and safe in the thought that a nurse would collect the baby first thing in the morning.

A wide path paved with cobbles led to the main door, which was simple and unadorned, without steps or portico. Inside the building the tiled floor, the shut windows, the bare walls reflected the distant voices of children whom she could not see. A nurse in a blue uniform, white pinafore and starched cap appeared in the corridor and surprised her with an inexplicable greeting: 'Nice to see you again, Sister.'

'I do not know you,' Sister María Inés said.

'We met last year.'

'I am afraid you are mistaken.'

'I still remember our discussion about the institution and the children.'

'You spoke to someone else. I have never been here before, Nurse.'

The woman wrinkled her brow. 'I apologise. Well, it's quite possible. It's your habit and veil. You all look alike. We nurses have the same problem.'

'Did someone visit you last year?' Sister María Inés asked. 'Someone like me – in a white habit?'

The nurse shrugged. 'I think so, yes. She never told me her name.'

Sister María Inés would have to think about that. Right now she wanted to look round the orphanage and the nurse was happy to give her a tour. She led the way down the corridor, the heavy bunch of keys that hung from her belt clinking with every step. Despite the hot summers, there were permanent damp patches on the walls and the ceiling. The signs of neglect and the indelible smell of carbolic soap were everywhere. In room after room there were rows of iron beds where young faces with hair cropped against lice peered at Sister María Inés. Guessing her thoughts the nurse said: 'We do all we can.' Sister María Inés nodded with secret satisfaction. What she saw strengthened her determination to keep the child. At the very least, in the convent he would be safe from disease. She knew the dangers of so many children living in a small space. Parasites and infectious diseases, dysentery, hepatitis . . . She had seen all that in Africa. The nurse was saying something but Sister María Inés paid no attention. She was thinking how she would teach Renato herself, at least until he was old enough to go to secondary school. She knew everything a child needed to learn – and there were books she could order by post.

They came back to the entrance and Sister María Inés stepped out into the light with relief. The nurse was still talking: '. . . which His Excellency was kind enough to donate. Next year we plan . . .' The Mother Superior excused herself and walked back towards the garage. Now the thought returned to her mind: who had visited the orphanage? All the nuns had been to the city at one time or another during the previous year. Perhaps it meant nothing, she thought: a nun on holiday from another diocese, or a visit by one of her nuns out of curiosity or the wish to make a donation, which the nun did not want the others to know about. She would have to think about that but now she had to hurry up. She missed the child. At the end of the road the garage had reopened after the afternoon siesta and the Ford was ready.

S ister Ana was very upset. She had expected the Bishop to
have ordered the Mother Superior to hand over the child
to the authorities by now. She did not understand why
the irrefutable evidence of satanic practices she had showed him
had caused him no alarm. After he had left the convent she
had returned to her room, dropped in bed and burst into tears
because he, the only person in the world whom she trusted,
had not believed her. She was certain of his kindness, admired
his intelligence, believed he was fair, and therefore she had to
blame herself for not having made him understand. She had
buried her head in her pillow and sobbed with frustration
because she knew that there was something evil about the child
in the suitcase even if she could not convince anyone else.

While she had sobbed she had realised that she was no longer
driven by her mistrust of the Mother Superior but by her deep faith
in God. She reproached herself for not having expected that her
task would be testing. She had to apply herself, observe carefully,
think very hard about how to solve the mystery, and only then
could she hope to defeat the demons that were laying siege to the
convent. And so she had stopped sobbing, wiped her tears and
begun: '*The Lord is my light and my salvation . . .*' She had prayed
gladly, and then had blown her nose on her sleeve and regained
her poise with the promise not to shed another tear until she
had triumphed over evil.

On her easel was a canvas she had started only days earlier,
Saint George slaying the dragon, but she was not in the mood
for painting. What she wanted to do was rest a little before
resuming her search for the truth about the child. She had just

lain down in bed when there was a knock on her door. Sister Teresa walked in.

'What do you want?' Sister Ana asked.

'I wanted to borrow the gramophone. I thought I could play my records.'

'The Mother might hear.'

'She's gone to the city.'

'No doubt to see His Excellency,' Sister Ana said.

Ever since the incident with the crying child, when the Mother Superior had chastised her for singing, Sister Teresa had not played her records, terrified that if the Mother Superior caught her again she would excommunicate her. Sister Ana waved her to the desk, where the gramophone was, but then changed her mind. 'No,' she said. 'Bring over your music instead.'

It had taken Sister Teresa years to build up her record collection with the money that the Mother Superior gave each nun every month, their share of the small profit from the selling of the altar breads. Sister Teresa returned a moment later with a stack of records, cranked the gramophone and took off her shoe to put her sock into the horn. Sister Ana said: 'You don't need that. No one will tell the Mother that you were playing music.'

The music sounded loud and melodic in the room with its bare walls. Sister Teresa tapped her feet to the rhythm and began to hum.

'If you want to sing, sing,' Sister Ana said. 'I don't mind.'

The other nun began to sing in a low voice. When the record ended, she asked Sister Ana for permission to put the needle back to the beginning and gave the crank a few turns. This time she sang better but still blushed with embarrassment, standing up with her eyes shut, imitating her musical idols, whose photographs she hid between the pages of her religious books. She had never sung popular songs in front of anyone before, only hymns in the chapel, but soon her embarrassment passed and she was pleased to have an audience. She asked for a little water, changed the record and started another song.

She believed that her voice was a gift from God and it would have been a sin not to use it, even if the words of her favourite songs were admittedly too bold to be uttered by a nun. She knew that she would never convince the Mother Superior but was happy that at least Sister Ana was on her side. She liked her for it, despite the woman's lack of humour, her meanness, her manic persecution of a little child who had no one in the world. Sister Teresa continued to sing as best she could, reaching the high notes without difficulty, switching with great ease from festive *bulerías* to solemn *malagueñas*.

Soon after the Mother Superior had left in the Ford that morning, it had begun to rain and it still had not stopped. The rain soaked the empty nests on the chimneys, turned the courtyard into a pool of muddy water and slaked the thirst of the dead waiting under the mossy gravestones of the convent cemetery for the Second Coming. Sister Ana listened to the songs. Although she did not approve of them, she said nothing. Sister Teresa finished a song and asked: 'Would you like to hear another, Sister?'

'Go ahead.'

The younger woman picked up another record from the stack, and Sister Ana went to the window. The courtyard was starting to flood. It would remain flooded most of the winter and when it snowed the rainwater would turn to thick ice. A nun with an umbrella passed under the window and crossed the courtyard, walking between the puddles. Sister Ana watched her indifferently. She felt something hit her cheek and looked above her head at the dripping ceiling. She put a bucket to catch the leak and the drops fell noisily in it. Music played on the gramophone and Sister Teresa continued to sing. Sister Ana concentrated her thoughts on the events of the previous weeks. She tried to remember everything that had happened from the moment the Mother Superior announced the discovery of the child on the steps of the convent: the old suitcase, the bloodied bed sheet, the mopped-up floor in a corner of the abandoned school for novices. She rearranged the events over and over again in her mind and tried to recall any peculiar incidents that had taken place days, weeks, even months before they had found the child . . . anything that might have been important. To her surprise it was not too difficult to do, for life in the convent was regimented with a simple routine that made it easy to identify any unusual event. While all that went on inside her mind, the lines on her forehead deepened and she held her breath. Then suddenly her eyes opened wide and she gave a loud gasp that made Sister Teresa stop in the middle of her song.

A few doors away Sister Beatriz had been swaddling the child when the music had begun. She recognised the flamencos of the placid Sundays from before the trouble began, when she used to sit at her desk reading while the notes from the muffled horn of the gramophone next door travelled into her room and dissolved the words of the Church Fathers she was trying to memorise. When she heard Sister Teresa's voice, hesitant and low, she was pleased: the convent was at last returning to some semblance of normality. She finished wrapping the child in the strips of cloth, covered him with a blanket and observed him with affection. The Mother Superior had not asked her opinion but Beatriz liked the name she had given him. She decided to take the child to listen to the music. She pulled up the blanket to cover the top of his head and left the room with him in her arms. She walked in the direction of the music but after a few steps understood that it was not coming from Sister Teresa's room but Sister Ana's. Disappointed because she knew that there was no way Sister Ana would let the child in, she turned back. At the refectory she picked up an umbrella and went for a walk with the child round the convent.

She crossed the courtyard under the rain, her shoes getting wet and the cold wind passing through her habit. She was confident that the Mother Superior would convince the Bishop to let them bring up the child in the convent. Renato coughed a couple of times and she wrapped him more tightly in the blanket. She took him to the garden, where the last flowers of the season were sinking into the mud, and passed near the spot where Sister Ana had found the buried bed sheet. On her way back from her walk, she heard the bell ringing for midday prayer.

It was time to feed the child. That morning the Mother Superior had instructed her to pray in her room and not take the child to the unheated chapel, where he might catch a cold. She would be angry if she found out that she had taken him for a walk in the rain. But it was not the first time that the young woman had disobeyed her: whenever she had the chance she did not feed him from the bowl. Today she did not have to worry about being caught. The Mother Superior was away and the sisters would be in the chapel. She waited until the prayers began and made her way to her room, where she placed the child in his cradle and then began to undress.

All that time Sister Ana had not stood idle. She was confident that she had found the answer to the riddle but wanted to keep it to herself. Ending the truce in her war against everyone, she dismissed Sister Teresa brusquely: 'Enough music for now. I have a serious matter to attend to.' When she was alone, she took another look at the bloodied bed sheet and could not believe that the truth which now seemed so obvious had not come to her earlier. She put the sheet away and went to the Mother Superior's room; she entered without knocking. Sister Beatriz and the child were not there. She looked for them in the refectory, the kitchen and the chapel but could not find them. She walked in the rain without an umbrella looking for the young nun until finally, when the bell rang for prayer, she caught a glimpse of Sister Beatriz going to her room with the child in her arms. Soaked by the rain, Sister Ana followed her from a distance. A moment later she was pushing open the door and the truth which she had guessed a little earlier was now confirmed: seated by the window and dressed only in her undergarment, Sister Beatriz was breastfeeding her child.

D espite her successful conjectures, which she had no doubt were the result of Divine Inspiration, Sister Ana never, in fact, managed to guess the whole truth. Its origins went back almost three years, when Bishop Estrada had decided to become confessor to the nuns of the convent of Our Lady of Mercy, not knowing that the Devil was setting him a trap. No one denied that he had a deep-seated faith in God and a great skill in diplomacy, which he had studied so carefully in his youth, but it was wrong of him to feel so confident of his own ability to fend off sin. In the event, evil did not ask him whether he truly believed in God or invite him to complex nego-tiations for his soul, but instead it struck him a single decisive blow when he least expected it.

The time he had spent with the deserter sentenced to death had shaken his belief in the natural kindness of the world and had set him off on a search for sanctuary. To counter his recur-rent sleeplessness, he took to carrying in a secret pocket inside his cassock a silver snuffbox filled with pills that made him shut his eyes the moment his head touched the pillow and sleep without interruption and without dreams. The problem was that he could only take them at night because they caused him to oversleep. And so his siestas remained an ordeal he had to endure awake every afternoon, when he undressed and lay in bed for a brief rest before returning to his desk. His bedroom was in a corner on the top floor of his palace. Both his offi-cial residence and the administrative seat of the diocese, the palace had windows that overlooked the river and the distant tiled roofs of the Orphanage of San Rafael the Healer, his proudest achievement. At its opening he had been asked to cut the ribbon in acknowledgement of his efforts, without which the orphanage would not have been built. Then he had delivered a passionate speech about the need for society not to turn its back on the innocent victims of its own recklessness, but to look after them with compassion and generosity. He had said: 'When people stop playing dice with human lives, there will no longer be a need for places like this. I pray that I am wrong, but fear that the moment will not come either in our or, alas, in God's lifetime.'

In the middle of the room was a big rococo bed made of Brazilian mahogany that still smelled of the jungle. It was the bed in which he was conceived, in which he was born and in which his parents had died quietly a few years apart of old age. Motivated less by sentimentality than the desperate hope of curing the torment of his siestas, Bishop Estrada had it brought over from his ancestral home and lay under its velvet canopy embroidered with the coat of arms of a family line that was bound to end with him. But the happy memories of his childhood preserved under the layers of varnish did not cure him. Without the sleeping pills to save him, he tossed and turned in the magnificent bed all afternoon and rose even more tired than when he had lain down. Unknown to everyone, he had begun to visit a hypnotist in the capital who tried to hypnotise him with a pendulum, but even though Bishop Estrada believed in modern science the treatment failed.

So when he started to go to the convent of Our Lady of Mercy, he was glad of the chance to leave the city of his afternoon ordeal and breathe the pure air of the mountains, but did not expect that in fact his Sundays there would turn out to be the answer to his prayers. Soon, to his great surprise, he discovered that his sleep became more peaceful, he rested well and his dreams were no longer the plaything of demons but had an innocence and optimism he had not felt in years. He was no longer miserable; he stopped taking the sleeping pills and looked forward to his monthly visits to the convent which had become his fountain of youth. He would arrive in his Model T Ford, one of the first to be shipped from America, and find the Mother Superior and the nuns waiting on the steps, alerted to his coming by the scared birds flying ahead of the explosions of the car exhaust. The women would wait with a jug of iced water, of which he would have several glassfuls before giving them his ring to kiss and entering the convent.

One Sunday morning, soon after he had appointed himself confessor to the nuns of the convent of Our Lady of Mercy, he set out from the city at the same time as always and in a good mood, looking forward to his visit. The car left behind the last vestiges of civilisation and began to climb the road used mostly by lumbermen who had transported wood from the forests since the age of the caravels. Wearing his coat, his airman's helmet and leather gloves, Bishop Estrada passed the monotony of the journey humming the songs of the *zarzuelas* by Amadeo Vives, Pablo Luna and Jacinto Guerrero, which were popular at that time all over the country and which one could not escape even in one's sleep. The cold wind beat against his face, the wheels bumped along the rough surface of the track and he was happy.

Some time later, as the Ford was coming out of a sharp bend, the engine puttered and gave out. Thinking that the car had just stalled on the uphill bend, he jumped out and gave the crank a turn. The engine did not start. He had tried the crank several times before he noticed, panting, that the radiator was leaking and when he looked inside he discovered that there were only a few drops of water left. Angry at himself for not having checked the car before setting out, he looked at his watch and guessed that he was closer to the convent than the city, although still a long way away.

The mishap had changed his mood and he no longer hummed as he walked in the direction of the convent. He was still far off when he saw someone on a donkey coming the other way. The animal was walking cautiously along the edge of the track while the rider, sitting side-saddle, was tapping it gently on with a switch. Sister Beatriz had seen him first and he had reminded her of a tireless and determined missionary plodding across some wilderness. She greeted him.

'At least Our Lord has answered my prayer in part,' the Bishop said. 'I had asked Him for a car mechanic.'

The nun got off the donkey and kissed his ring. 'We were very worried about you,' she said and fetched her canteen from the saddle. While taking a few dignified sips of water, the Bishop looked in the direction he had come from. 'Perhaps the radiator would not have rusted if I filled it with holy water,' he said. 'Are we far from the convent?'

Sister Beatriz nodded. 'Do not worry, Your Excellency. You will ride.'

The Bishop glanced at the old donkey. 'Fine,' he said. 'But only half the journey, Sister. Then promise me that we will swap.'

He gathered up his coat and cassock, sat on the donkey and looked at his feet with amusement: they almost reached the ground. He patted the animal's head, and the donkey swung its tail a couple of times like a greeting. 'What is its name?'

'Midas.'

'Of course,' the Bishop said. 'He bears an obvious resemblance.'

They set out, Bishop Estrada holding onto the pommel and Sister Beatriz walking a few steps ahead of him. It was almost midday in early spring, already warm in the lowlands, where he had begun his journey that morning but still cold in the mountains, where life was only beginning to awake from a deep winter. There was a little snow on the highest peaks of the sierra but none on its forested slopes, which resonated with birdsong. A short while later, as they rounded another bend and the landscape opened up, there was a view of the interminable plain very far away, gleaming in the sunlight, a patchwork of green and brown fields. The Bishop stood mesmerised by its immensity until the track changed direction again, and animal and humans continued their ascent with their backs to the plain. It had been impossible to notice any of this on his previous journeys behind the clouds of dust, the noise and the smell of petrol. Shivering a little inside his coat, Bishop Estrada observed the young woman. He said: 'Remind me of your name, Sister.'

'Beatriz, Your Excellency.'

'Where do you come from?'

'Far from here.'

'Everywhere is far from here,' the Bishop said light-heartedly. 'Is it colder than this?'

'Yes.'

'Then you must come from the North Pole.'

They said nothing else until they arrived at the convent late in the afternoon. The nuns received him with great shows of joy, kissing his ring and asking what had happened to him, offering him glasses of water, plates of fruit, handkerchieves sprinkled with eau de cologne to hold under his nose, cold compresses to place on his forehead in case he had suffered a heatstroke, despite it being a cold April day. Tired from the journey, Bishop Estrada said: 'Enough, Sisters, please. I think you mistake me for the Messiah because I came on the donkey.'

Then he remembered that he had not switched places with Sister Beatriz during the ride. 'Thank you for your deceit, Sister,' he told her. 'But if we make any agreement again, promise me to honour it.'

His room had been prepared but he did not wish to rest and went straight to the chapel to hear confessions while there was still light. He had suggested that the women should always draw lots to decide the order in which they would come to confession. The system he had devised meant that he did not know who was speaking to him from the other side of the lattice and the nuns would feel freer to speak without qualms, without fear and without shame. The only voice he thought he recognised was the Mother Superior's.

Later, at the altar, he felt a nervousness he had not felt since the early days of his priesthood, when he occasionally celebrated Mass while still a student of ecclesiastical diplomacy. He now did his duty without difficulty but could not stop wondering why he felt this way. He could only attribute it to his tiredness after the biblical journey on the donkey. Whenever he turned away from the altar to face his small congregation, his eyes sought, as if of their own volition, the young woman who had come to his rescue earlier that day.

It was almost evening when the Mass ended and it was too cold to eat outside. The Mother Superior invited the Bishop to have dinner in the refectory. The food had long gone cold but he insisted that he did not wish it warmed up. He ate without appetite, keeping his eyes fixed on his plate while repeating his regular jokes, which, no matter how many times he said them, never seemed to lose their ability to entertain. He finished his food before everyone else and declined the repeated offers of a second helping. Sister María Inés escorted him to her room for their customary discussion about the affairs of the convent and his last cup of coffee before leaving for the city. It was almost dark when she opened the ledger where all the business matters of the convent were recorded. 'I am afraid you will have to stay the night, Your Excellency,' she said. 'It is impossible to take you to your car in the dark.'

The Bishop, grateful for her hospitality, accepted. He sipped at his coffee, paying no attention to the ledger. 'That sister of yours,' he said, after a while.

The Mother Superior raised her eyes from the book.

'The one who came in search of me with the donkey earlier today,' the Bishop continued. 'She was extremely kind to let me ride all the way.'

'She has not been here very long. Beatriz came shortly before we lost our old confessor. So far I am very pleased with her. She is very capable. She could well become my successor.'

The Bishop asked no more questions but leaned over the ledger and pretended to listen while the Mother Superior went through the accounts line by line. When she finished, more than an hour later, he asked for a lamp to light his way to the guesthouse and said goodnight, promising the Mother Superior to say Mass again the following morning before returning to the city. Although he was very tired, he slept very little. He lay in bed watching the moon through the windows, listening to an owl hidden in the roof and thinking of the young nun. He regretted no longer carrying the snuffbox with the sleeping pills. A little before dawn he finally drifted off and dreamed of the young nun coming to his room. She wore a loose nightdress, which she unbuttoned standing in the middle of the room and let it drop like a feather to the floor before joining him under the covers. Not long afterwards the first shafts of sunlight woke him up with a sudden jolt. Full of remorse for his impure dream, he knelt and prayed with his eyes shut, hoping that his having yielded to temptation in his sleep would be the end of it. But in his most secret and true thoughts he already knew that it was merely the beginning.

Bishop Estrada managed to resist the temptation long enough to admit to himself that sooner or later he would succumb to it. The irony of his situation did not escape him. Although he turned a blind eye to the cases where priests in his diocese shared their bed with a woman (as long as they always shared it with the same one, she was unmarried and both were discreet about it), he took pride in thinking that his armour was impenetrable to the pleasures of the flesh. When he returned to the city from the convent, he reread Saint Augustine, whom he had not read since adolescence and had been an inspiration to him, with the hope that he would help him out of his quandary. This time, in his middle age, he read him without the idealism of his youth, the absolute conviction, the yearning for the martyrdom of celibacy, but with the sad wisdom of an older man no longer capable of such heartless emotions. Consequently, he found nothing in Saint Augustine that was helpful. Unable to put the young woman out of his mind, he went for long walks in the gardens of his palace. The skirt of his cassock was constantly caught in the thorns of the rose bushes, leaving behind a trail of perfumed red petals which hours later his deacon had only to follow to find him seated on a stone bench, distant and thoughtful, as if he were praying.

All this time Sister Beatriz knew nothing about the Bishop's suffering. Most of what had happened on their fateful encounter on the road to the convent had already faded from her memory when months later she entered the chapel. That Sunday the Mother Superior had invited the Bishop to have lunch before carrying out his pastoral duties. The meal under the vine had been a languid affair with battered fish, followed by plates of candied almonds for the nuns and glasses of red wine with lemonade and ice for him. It was late afternoon when the women began to come to confession. When Sister Beatriz's turn came, it was almost evening and she had to light a candle to find her way to the confessional. She had finished her confession and stood up to go when the Bishop unexpectedly spoke to her through the lattice: 'Is that you, Sister Beatriz?'

The nun paused with the candle in her hand. 'Yes, Your Excellency.'

'Ah, I thought so,' the voice on the other side of the lattice said. 'I recognised your voice.'

She stood uncomfortably in the narrow confessional as if she were listening to a stranger. The voice that moments earlier had said with gentleness and authority '*Ego te absolvo a peccatis tuis,*' now had a different tone. She opened the door of the cubicle but did not step out, getting the impression that she had not been given permission to go yet. A little cool air blew into the small space where she had knelt reciting her venial sins. She waited for the voice to speak again. Outside the sun set and the courtyard turned dark and quiet. The other nuns, having made their confessions before her, were in the refectory waiting for the Bishop to call them to evening Mass. One of Sister Carlota's stray dogs, still alive back then, sensed the human presence in the chapel and stood at the door sniffing the air. The voice close to Sister Beatriz said gently: 'In fact I suspected it was you from the moment you came into the chapel. I recognised the sound of your feet but I was not completely certain. Are you the last sister to confession today?'

The woman said that she was. The dog went away. The Bishop

spoke again through the lattice in a weary voice: 'Let us talk a little.'

Sister Beatriz closed the door on her side of the confessional and knelt down on the cushion again – there was no proper seat in the cubicle, only the kneeler. The candle flickered in the draught and her shadow fell over the four wooden panels surrounding her before it settled behind her. The voice asked: 'Do you know my name, Sister Beatriz?'

'Estrada, Your Excellency.'

'No, my Christian name.'

'I don't know it, Your Excellency.'

'Ezequiel. Everyone knows who I am but very few know my Christian name.' He gave a chuckle. 'I am afraid I didn't put enough lemonade in my wine today. I had too much to drink.'

The nun knelt in silence while on the other side of the lattice the voice continued: 'Listen, Beatriz. For months I tried . . . Do you understand? I have been . . .' It hesitated. 'Oh God, forgive me.'

'I should go back, Your Excellency.'

'Put out your candle, please. My eyes hurt. Maybe it is the wine. Put it out.'

'Someone might come,' the woman said weakly and heard the door on the other side of the confessional open. Time passed and nothing happened while she waited, kneeling on the cushion and holding her breath, for the door on her side to open too. The Bishop spoke from outside: 'Put out the candle, please.' She made no reply, holding the candle tightly with both hands, but slowly she stopped being afraid and an almost motherly feeling came over her. There was a timid knock on the door and the voice said again: 'Put out the candle. Spare me the . . .' Then a great force of compassion free of fear or shame lifted her from the kneeler. For a moment her shadow fluttered over the vaulted ceiling of the chapel, and then she took a deep breath and blew out the candle.

The first thing that they agreed was not to let passion stand in the way of their good sense but to take every care not to raise the slightest suspicion. Their best defence was the boundless adulation of the nuns of Our Lady of Mercy for the Bishop, whom they thought incapable even of the most trivial sin. Nevertheless he insisted that they were never to be seen speaking in private, even if Sister Beatriz had something innocent to tell him. When their paths crossed in the convent, she only bowed to him and he greeted her with a hardly noticeable movement of his hand before they went their separate ways. He never lost his head in the confessional again or spoke about what had happened, but met her in his room in the guesthouse, where he began to spend the night during his monthly visits, professing to be exhausted from his drive to the mountains.

Once he had retired to his room he waited for her without taking off his clothes. Some time later, which always felt like eternity to him, there was a coded knock on the door and he immediately put out the light. Having removed her shoes so as not to make any noise, she came in like a cat, and without either of them saying a word she searched for his shadow in the dark and began to undress him. She started with his pectoral cross, which glimmered in the moonlight, and at those moments it felt to him unbearably heavy with the weight of his sin. After she had gently removed it from around his neck, she unwrapped his purple sash and undid the thirty-three buttons of his cassock.

On one occasion they were almost caught. Sister Beatriz was about to leave the Bishop's room in the middle of the night when one of the dogs that happened to sleep outside the door barked at her. She shut the door again and heard footsteps not far away. The bell rang for nocturns: she had forgotten it was time for prayers. Behind her, the Bishop, who was as terrified as she was, heaved a sigh of relief. 'At least God has not condemned us,' he said.

'No,' Sister Beatriz said. 'It's the dogs which are on our side.'

They agreed that he should no longer stay the night in the convent. Bishop Estrada thought that it would be safer if she visited him when she came to the city to buy provisions for the convent, a duty which the four younger nuns (Sister Carlota was too old to make the journey on the donkey) took in turns. So, once a month, Sister Beatriz left the convent immediately after the dawn prayer and almost five hours later arrived in the city, where she spent the morning in the market. After filling Midas's panniers she headed for the square in front of the Bishop's Palace, and there she walked up and down, waiting for the secret signal. When Bishop Estrada was ready for her, he came to the window of his office and opened and closed the drapes twice. Then she made her way to the quiet cobbled alley round the back of the palace and a little while later the Bishop came to let her into the garage, where she tied Midas next to the Ford. A spiral staircase led directly to his private quarters.

There they did not have to worry. Bishop Estrada had given strict instructions not to be disturbed during his siesta, even if the palace caught fire. After they had made love, he escorted her back down the stairs and let her out of the garage with the only key, which he kept in his pocket at all times. The woman left without kisses or goodbyes, pulling the lead-rope of the donkey and raising no suspicions in her religious habit. Later, when the Bishop bought a new car, he donated the old Ford to the convent and Sister Beatriz was able to meet with him with greater ease and more often but still in secret.

Things would have stayed the way they were if she had not

become pregnant. Sister Beatriz, who knew all along that the Bishop would not tolerate a pregnancy, decided not to tell him. He often warned her that a child would seal their damnation and he made a point of always wearing a condom. Sister Beatriz assumed that he had an accomplice who bought them for him, but one day Bishop Estrada asked her to follow him to the basement of the palace, where he showed her several old crates that contained hand-dipped vulcanised-rubber condoms made by Julius Schmid, Inc. at the turn of the century. They were what had been left of one of his many enlightened schemes that over the years had landed him in trouble with the Vatican. He had bought them at trade price with the intention of distributing them for free across his diocese, convinced that they would stem the spread of syphilis, which still claimed many lives, but a delegation of parish priests got wind of his 'moral prophylaxis' scheme and wrote to the Holy See. He was duly reprimanded and so he was left with enough condoms to sin his way to the ninth circle of Hell.

The pregnancy made Sister Beatriz face up to her situation. She never thought of not having the baby because to her that would have been a far greater sin than the one she was already committing, but she understood that she risked being expelled from the convent and that the Bishop could be defrocked. She did not want to leave the Order or destroy him. If she went somewhere to give birth she would have to give the baby away to be able to return to Our Lady of Mercy. She thought about it for several days and came up with a way of having the child in the convent while at the same time saving both the Bishop and herself from excommunication.

The first thing she had to do was end the affair before he noticed the change in her body. It was a difficult decision because all this time he had given her no reason to leave him, but she took comfort from knowing that her plan would not only save the child and herself from destitution but also the Bishop from disgrace. She still loved him: she loved the way he talked to her; she loved his indomitable spirit, his passion for philanthropy and his well-intentioned but doomed schemes; she loved the fact that after they had made love his member smelled of vulcanised rubber, which he tried to drive away with scalding baths and carbolic soap. But she had to leave him. Afraid of how he might react, she did not end their affair in the city but chose to tell him in the confessional the next time he came to the convent. Without tears, she tried to convince him that it was the right thing to do, giving him several reasons why: they were condemning their souls, they were risking being caught, she was losing interest in the act of love. She told him anything but the truth. Bishop Estrada listened in silence until she finished and then said from the other side of the confessional: 'Go. I cannot stop you. You do not have to pretend to be the Virgin.'

They were his last words on the matter. Since then he gave every sign that he had forgotten about her. He did not try to dissuade her, did not address her when he sat at lunch with the nuns during his visits, did not come out of the confessional until she had left the chapel. Soon she was too occupied with how to deceive everyone about her pregnancy to think of anything else. Her plan was to pass the baby off as an orphan and have the nuns adopt him so that she would not have to part from him. She had decided to keep him after a visit to the orphanage of San Rafael the Healer, where she had been appalled by the overcrowding of the wards. It was her visit the nurse remembered when, months later, Sister María Inés also happened to come to the orphanage.

In any case, Sister Beatriz sewed a habit several sizes larger than her current one to hide the way her belly would grow over the next months, and bought an old suitcase which she lined with cotton wool, having had the idea after seeing the night depository for babies at the orphanage. The old school for novices was a good place to give birth in secret because no one went in for fear that it might collapse. She cleaned and prepared a corner in one of the upstairs rooms and prayed for an easy labour. As her time approached she had to ask to be excused from driving the Ford to the city, and when the day came, she went to the derelict building at the very last moment and delivered the baby after a short labour whose worst part was her fear of someone suddenly turning up. Then, exhausted, she bathed the baby and wrapped him up, mopped the floor and buried the bloodied bed sheet on which she had lain to give birth in a secluded corner of the grounds. Early the following morning, while the other sisters were at prayer, she put the newborn in the old suitcase and left him on the steps at the entrance to the convent, where later Sister Lucía came across him on her way to the car.

The Bishop's bitterness towards Sister Beatriz concealed a sadness which still showed no signs of waning several months after she had ended their love affair. His visits to the convent became an ordeal of pretences and evasions until, having no more patience left, he made the decision to appoint another priest in his place. He had to find someone who was not only willing to travel to that corner of the diocese several times a year but who was also in no risk of falling into the trap the Bishop had fallen into himself. No parish priest he offered the post wished to do it, claiming that they were too busy already, so he tried the seminary, where he hoped that the idealism of youth would provide him with the appropriate candidate. He interviewed several seminarians, all of them keen to serve under his command, ruled out both those physically unfit for such an arduous duty and the handsome ones, who might cause other kinds of trouble, and settled on Mateo, a timid young man who impressed him with the humility of his pitted face.

Bishop Estrada did not have the slightest suspicion that the nun was pregnant. He assumed that Sister Beatriz continued to come to the city in the Ford once a week to buy provisions, and still hoped against hope that one day she might visit him again. She never did, but this did not deter him from standing at the big windows of his office several times a day and gazing out at the square with the statue of San Rafael, where she used to wait for his signal.

A few days after his reluctant visit to the convent, where he had gone to investigate the matter of the orphan, he looked out of the window in his usual, sad, half-hearted way and saw a nun in a white habit and black veil striding across the square. Immediately he felt that the prophecy of his lover's return, in which he so desperately believed, was at long last being fulfilled. Forgetting his bitterness, he began to make the signal, opening and closing the curtains until the nun got closer and he saw, to his horror, that it was not Sister Beatriz but that unpleasant woman Sister Ana. He let go of the drapes and walked away from the window feeling annoyed. When his deacon came in to announce her, Bishop Estrada answered before the young man had a chance to speak: 'Send her in.'

A moment later Sister Ana greeted him with a mischievous smile. 'Your Excellency,' she said. 'I saw you standing at the window.'

'Did you?'

'Yes. I could tell it was you from the other end of the square. You were doing something with the curtains.'

Bishop Estrada pouted. 'Ah yes. I was only trying . . .' He made a dismissive gesture in the direction of the window he had been standing at earlier. 'The drapes were stuck. The rail is prob-- ably bent.'

Reminding himself that he was not obliged to explain himself to a nun, he stopped and stared at her with a serious expression. He could tell that she was very excited about something.

'Did you smuggle yourself out of the convent again, Sister?' he asked.

The nun giggled. 'Oh no, Your Excellency, not this time. I came in the car with Sister Lucía. She is at the market.'

The Bishop asked: 'Not with Sister Beatriz?'

'Not this time. She has been helping the Mother with the baby.' She giggled again, oblivious to the Bishop's severe look. 'Who would have thought?' she said. 'It's quite unbelievable.'

'Does whatever you find unbelievable have anything to do with me?'

'Yes, Your Excellency, very much so. It's Sister Beatriz I came to talk to you about.'

The Bishop went red in the face. All sorts of thoughts ran through his mind as he slowly went up to the window and looked out with his hands clasped behind his back. 'Very well, Sister,' he said harshly. 'Speak your piece.'

He expected the nun to tell him that she knew about Sister Beatriz and him, but what he heard shocked him more: Sister Beatriz was the mother of the child. He said: 'Impossible.'

'She admitted it to me, Your Excellency.'

Bishop Estrada observed her with dismay, trying to determine whether she suspected him of being the father. Several minutes passed in silence before he spoke up: 'Who else knows?'

'No one, Your Excellency. I discovered it the day the Mother visited you.'

'Do you think she plays a part in all this?'

'I doubt it. Sister Beatriz begged me not to tell her.'

Bishop Estrada calmed down a little. He said: 'Promise me not to say anything about this to anyone.'

'Of course, Your Excellency.'

'No one – do you understand? I will take care of it. We have to avoid a scandal. These things can harm the Church more than anything else. We have to protect our faith.'

'I will do whatever you say.'

'Good. I appreciate your help, Sister. Naturally you will be rewarded for your loyalty.' He searched for a better word. 'And your vigilance, of course,' he finally said, holding back his contempt.

'I do not expect anything in return.'

'I believe we once discussed the post of sister visitatrix.'

'Yes, Your Excellency, we did. It would be an honour to accept it with great humility.'

'Let us sort out this mess first.'

Bishop Estrada saw her out and then gave orders not to be disturbed. Shut away in his office, he spared a moment to question how such an accident could have happened when he had taken every precaution, and only then did it strike him as very reckless to have put his faith in a piece of rubber almost thirty years old. He tried to think of a way to save himself from the scandal while causing the least harm to Sister Beatriz, and decided that the best thing he could do was to safeguard his own integrity in order to help the woman and her child as best he could.

Early that evening his deacon knocked on the door but received no reply. He assumed the Bishop had already gone to his room, so he finished his paperwork and left too. It was almost night-time when Bishop Estrada came out of his daze and answered the knock on the door as if he had just heard it: 'Come in, Ignacio.' No one answered and he went next door, where he did not find his secretary at his desk. The waiting room was dark and quiet, and he shuddered as if he were alone not just in the building but in the whole city. He had repeatedly refused the services of a live-in housekeeper and told the cook and servants to always go home as soon as they finished their tasks, for he wanted to keep up some pretence of the simple life that suits a good Christian. He now went from room to room without turning the lights on, bumping into the furniture like a ghost not yet accustomed to its eternal night. The pale moonlight through the windows lit up the portraits of the bishops with the heavy jowls who had served God before him and were now buried under the cold flagstones of the great cathedral. He finally found his way to his bedroom and prayed to God to help him out of his quandary. He said: 'I was aware of the sin that I was committing and I have no right to ask You for clemency. But please spare me the ridicule and let me serve You until the end of my days before You decide what to do with me.' Then he offered a way to atone for his mistake: 'I will do all I can for that child.'

He finished his prayer and lay exhausted in bed but found it impossible to sleep. He left in the car before dawn and arrived at the convent as the nuns were coming out of the early morning prayer. The Mother Superior said: 'Welcome, Your Excellency. We did not expect you.' But the Bishop's solemn expression made her worry and she added: 'I hope you are a bringer of good news.'

'My visit is connected of course with the matter of the orphan,' the Bishop said. 'I would like a word with Sister Beatriz and you, but separately.'

He took off his leather helmet and followed Sister María Inés to her office, looking tired after his sleepless night and the car journey. The convent had lost all its charm for him and seemed no more than a few derelict buildings at the mercy of time. He walked across the courtyard hoping he would never have to visit again. In the room kept warm for the child's sake by a petrol heater, he took off his coat and handed it together with his helmet to the Mother Superior. She hung them behind the door as if she were handling sacred relics, then sat opposite him. Bishop Estrada glanced at the cradle in the corner, where the baby was stirring noiselessly, and turned to Sister María Inés. He said: 'I wish to speak to Sister Beatriz first.'

She called the young nun and left the room. When Sister Beatriz came in, the Bishop said, without looking at her: 'Shut the door and take a seat.'

She obeyed. Then he began, still not looking at her. 'We have a problem on our hands. And I know that I am responsible at least as much as you are.'

'I do not understand, Your Excellency.'

'Please,' the Bishop said. 'This is not necessary. Sister Ana came to see me yesterday.'

The nun looked at him coldly and said: 'I assume you have told the Mother.'

'I have told no one. I want you to know that I am on your side.'

'How can you persuade Sister Ana to keep quiet?'

'With bribery.' He waved his hand. 'Do not worry about her.'

He left the desk and walked up to the cradle. Observing the child, he resisted the temptation to deny that he was the father; it would have been vile. He said: 'Remind me of his name.'

'Renato. The Mother had him baptised.'

'I know, I know.' The Bishop sighed deeply and said: 'You should have told me, but I understand why you did not. We have to make arrangements.'

'I want to keep him.'

'I am prepared to take care of him. I will do everything that is necessary. Your name will not be mentioned. No one else needs to know. We only have to adhere to the facts.'

'The facts?'

'The fact is that the child was found on the steps of the convent. Nothing will change. You will be able to go on with your life here. No reason to worry about Sister Ana. She is prepared to go to the Moon if she is given a senior appointment.'

'Will they take Renato to the orphanage?'

'Yes. Do you mean the one in the city? No . . . Yes, to start with, of course. Those will be the people who will come to collect him. But then we have to find a better place for him. I will find the best institution in the country and make sure that he gets a good education.'

'I want to be able to see him.'

'It will not be possible. He will be registered as an orphan.' Bishop Estrada felt his Roman collar soaked in sweat. He showed her out, saying, 'I am afraid it is the only possible solution. And then we may be able to make our peace with God.'

He still had to speak to the Mother Superior. He knew that it would be much harder to persuade her, but at least it was not necessary for his plan that he did. Sister María Inés came in looking worried. She said: 'Beatriz seems very distressed, Your Excellency.'

'Did she say anything to you?'

'No. She was almost in tears.'

The Bishop puffed. 'If I were Solomon I would give each of you half of that blessed child. The way things are I am sorry to inform you that I have decided to notify the orphanage.'

Sister María Inés's face hardened. 'You had given me to understand that you were in favour of us keeping him, Your Excellency.'

'That was your interpretation, Sister. All I said was that I reserved judgement.'

'Our faith demands that we offer our love and help to everyone and not pass the responsibility on to others.'

'I do not need more catechism lessons, Sister. I had enough in Rome a long time ago and from better teachers.'

'A long time ago, yes. Perhaps that is why you appear to have forgotten them, Your Excellency.'

The Bishop tapped his foot and spoke calmly. 'Be careful what you say. Your commendable kindness aside, you propose something that is both illegal and improper. A convent is not the place to bring up a boy.'

'Why not, if that is what God wishes? His coming here is nothing less than a miracle.'

'Well, it is nice of you to say so, but I suspect we can find a simpler explanation without having to resort to metaphysics. After all, miracles happen very rarely but babies are being abandoned all the time.'

'But not here – why *here*? We are so many miles from anywhere.'

The Bishop shrugged. 'That I do not know. Perhaps it was a penance to Our Lady of Mercy – or somebody who could not afford to be seen leaving it at the orphanage. But she trusted the nuns to be kind to it.' He stopped before his suggestions came closer to the truth.

'One way or another, it's a miracle,' Sister María Inés said. 'If only I could tell you what I know you would have no difficulty believing me.'

'Please tell me,' the Bishop said with a sigh.

Sister María Inés shook her head. 'I do not wish to speak about it.' She pulled a handkerchief from her sleeve and wiped her eyes. 'I apologise for my behaviour.'

'I do not blame you. I will make sure they take good care of him.'

Bishop Estrada glanced at his watch: he had to return to the city. The Mother Superior fetched his coat and helmet, and he followed her out to his car. The other nuns joined them to wave him goodbye. Pleased with his diplomatic skills, he cranked the engine with a strength that surprised him and sat behind the wheel. He thought that his discussions with Sister Beatriz and the Mother Superior had gone better than he expected. He put on his leather helmet, turned the car round and smiled first at Sister Beatriz, then at Sister María Inés, without the least inkling that it was the last time he would see either of them.

Sister María Inés could not tell the Bishop what had happened in her youth, even though she was confident that it would have explained her behaviour and made him understand that the arrival of the orphan was not an event determined by a throw of the dice but the outcome of Divine Grace: her ultimate forgiveness after decades of constant penance. But the fact was that she had committed a mortal sin which carried an automatic sentence of excommunication, and the Bishop would be obliged to remove her from her position as mother superior and revoke all her other rights and privileges. She could still go to Mass but would be forbidden from leading the prayers and receiving the sacraments. More importantly, someone else would be put in charge of the convent and then she, Sister María Inés, would no longer have the power to protect the child. So she kept quiet, admitting to herself that one day she would have to confess her sin, as her faith and conscience obliged her to do, but promising to do it and face the consequences only when Renato was old enough not to need her any more. For now she had to carry on living in the shadow of her act.

As to the Bishop's conduct, his demand that she surrender the child to the authorities had come as a shock to her because he had led her to expect the opposite decision. Sister María Inés thought that he had deliberately deceived her and she no longer trusted or respected him. She revised her opinion of him and began to think of him as a vain man instead of a humble servant of God and a radical reformer: he was a scheming manipulator, a cruel diplomat who owed his success only to his affluent upbringing and his family connections. She could not believe that she had been taken in by him for so long. A feeling of bitterness came over her as she recalled the once pleasant memories of his visits and easily found fault with everything about him: his lunchtime jokes that verged on the immoral, his healthy appetite, his regular haircuts, his manicured hands, his handkerchiefs sprinkled with eau de cologne made in Paris. These things did not belong to a virtuous man. Now she scrutinised every incident involving him that she could remember, every gesture of his, every comment that unmasked the truth of his wickedness. Once, for example, he had said during lunch: 'Those who experience temptation merit our wholehearted admiration.' The nuns had been baffled by his remark until he had explained: 'Because only they know how Our Lord felt in the Garden of Gethsemane.' Sister María Inés had thought nothing of his remark then, but now she interpreted it as nothing less than a blatant encouragement for the sisters to commit sin.

When Bishop Estrada had told her what he had decided to do with the child, she had held her peace but had no intention of obeying him. She instantly knew that she had to take Renato away from the convent before the people from the orphanage came. She escorted the Bishop back to his car, waved goodbye to him despite seething with indignation and then went to the kitchen to prepare the child's milk. Gradually her decision to abandon the convent lightened her mood. After more than thirty years of having served God and nursed a sadness which until recently she believed incurable, she was ready again to face the world for which she had nothing but scorn. It was out there that she had undergone a medical procedure in secret, had been separated from her fiancé, had witnessed human suffering while a missionary: a world capable of great evil. If she had not joined the convent, she thought, she would have never found her way out of her predicament but would have continued to live in the labyrinth until the end of her life.

She had no doubt it was God's will that she should now return to it. But she would miss opening her eyes before the first light of dawn, getting out of bed and dressing in the dark with the care of a blind person: the white tunic and scapular, the leather belt, the black cape, the black veil, kissing every item before putting it on. Then she would go down on her knees and say the rosary, facing the wall that was hung with the pictures of the saints and the portrait of the young naval cadet. And she would miss the coldness of her room, its damp walls, the warped wooden floors that it made her seasick to walk across, the cloud of downy white feathers that blew in through the window from the storks' nests on the chimneys.

She returned to her room with the bowl of milk, fed the child, then went for a walk round the convent cradling him in her arms. She was determined to go the following morning without telling anyone, not even Sister Beatriz, who had been on her side all this time, for this was a matter that concerned her own destiny and no one else's. She hoped to find work under another name as a nurse in a hospital far away. She looked for a last time at the statues with the enigmatic faces in the cloister, the bell tower, the cemetery carpeted with autumn leaves, the irreparable decay that was everywhere and had cloaked her guilt all those years in its fragrant mist. In the car shed she hung the nosebag around Midas's head, then checked the Ford. She topped up the water and the oil, filled the tank and put the jerrycan with the rest of the petrol in the back seat. She worked calmly, the door of the shed left wide open to allow the light in, unafraid that someone might see her. They would suspect nothing because servicing the Ford was her favourite pastime.

She was in the chapel in time for the midday prayer and then joined the nuns at lunch in the refectory. Sister Ana was also at the table after a very long absence. The Mother Superior winced at this proclamation of victory but said nothing. She ate without paying any attention to the reading, which that day she found dull, and thought about her plan. When she finished her meal, she waited until everyone had finished too and then made a surprising announcement. 'Sister Teresa,' she said with the faintest trace of a smile, 'it is about time I had a look at your records.'

And so it was revealed that she had known for a long time about Sister Teresa's habit of playing the songs of the gypsies despite the sock pushed into the gramophone horn, but she had never said so because the music reminded her of the Edison phonograph of her youth. A moment later Sister Teresa returned with her records and the gramophone. She asked: 'Now what, Mother?'

'Now we listen to music,' Sister María Inés replied.

Sister Teresa put on her favourite record and turned the handle. When the needle reached the end, the Mother Superior asked the woman to play another record and then another, and listened tapping her fingers on the table. None of the other women sitting around the table could grasp the significance of that moment: it was a ceremony, as sacred as any Mass, to mark Sister María Inés's imminent return to the world.

After she had listened to all the records from beginning to end, Sister María Inés knelt in front of the Jesus on the Cross and left the refectory. She went straight to her room, and took out the suitcase which she would only pack when it was time to visit the Superioress General in the capital. She was still packing when later that evening Sister Beatriz knocked on her door. The Mother Superior hid the suitcase under her bed before giving the nun permission to enter. Sister Beatriz came in and asked: 'How is the child, Mother?'

'He will need his milk soon.'

'What did His Excellency say to you?'

The Mother Superior rocked the cradle and replied while looking at the child: 'Everything will be fine. We have won. Renato can stay.'

'I don't understand. His Excellency told me that he wanted the child taken to an orphanage far from here.'

'Far from here? What is wrong with the one in the city?' Sister María Inés asked and bent down to pick up the child. 'In any case I persuaded him that the best thing for Renato is to stay with us. It was not easy, of course. You know that His Excellency has studied diplomacy in Rome.'

Sister Beatriz was surprised as much by the news as by the Mother Superior's great calmness. 'When I left your room, I had the impression that the matter was closed,' she said.

'No matter is closed if you have faith,' Sister María Inés said. 'And persistence of course.'

'It is unbelievable. His Excellency spoke to me with great conviction.'

Sister María Inés gave the young nun a look of disapproval. 'It seems to me that you do not believe me, Beatriz.'

The nun stood in the middle of the room, saying nothing.

'Don't just stand there,' Sister María Inés said. 'Aren't you happy to hear the news?'

'I hope His Excellency will not change his mind.'

'He will not. Bring me some milk.'

When Sister Beatriz returned with the milk, the Mother Superior took it and sent her away. After she had fed the child and put him to sleep, she went back to packing her suitcase.

There were very few clothes that she could take, for she had used the old dresses in her cedar chest, whose airtight lid had kept the smells of her ill-fated courtship alive all those years, to make clothes for the baby. When everything was finally done, she lay in bed, too tired to take off her habit, and fell asleep almost at once. During the night she left her bed to go to nocturns before the bell had even rung, obeying a routine that had become an instinct to her. She made her way to the chapel, led the prayer and returned to her room like a sleepwalker. She fell into a deep sleep again and dreamed that she had died and was lying on the table in the refectory. The sisters were all there around the table, together with the Bishop and Father Mateo, but instead of performing the last rites they were dancing to the music on the gramophone. Later, with the music still playing, they carried her to the woods, opened the hole where the poisoned dogs were buried and threw her in among the rotting carcasses.

She woke up sometime before dawn with the music still ringing in her ears, unable to understand her macabre dream. There was no time to think about it – she had to leave. She lit the candle at her bedside and pulled out the suitcase from under the bed. But when she went to take the child from the cradle she saw that he was missing.

It was still night outside with only a thin crescent moon, but she did not need much light to find her way in the dark. She had walked countless times to the chapel in the middle of the night and knew well every corner of the convent. She did not think to take her lamp but ran out of her room and climbed down the stairs, two steps at a time. Before reaching the ground floor, she stepped on her habit and fell down several steps, grazing her ankle where the dog had bitten her. She felt a sharp pain but quickly stood up and went on, panting and holding up the train of her habit, so as not to trip over it again. At the far end of the cloister she climbed the stairs and went across the loggia to the last door. She threw it open and entered the room. For a moment she could make out nothing, but slowly her eyes became accustomed to the dark, and she began to see the easel, the table with the jars of pigments, the brushes. On the bed something shifted under the covers, and when she hit it with her fist she heard a muffled cry.

'Wake up,' she said.

Sister Ana opened her eyes, terrified by the hit in the dark.

'Tell me where the child is,' Sister María Inés said.

The other woman tried to hide under the covers again. 'Go away,' she said. 'You are controlled by the evil spirits.'

'Answer me!' Sister María Inés screamed.

When the other sisters heard the screams, they came to the door with their lamps. The Mother Superior ordered them to light the room so that she could search it. She looked everywhere but nothing seemed out of the ordinary. Then she saw that Sister Beatriz was not among the women. No one knew where she was.

Sister María Inés quickly went to the young nun's room. The bed was made with fresh sheets, while the cold air from the open windows had long cleared the warmth and odour of human presence. On the table, next to a pile of books from the convent library, a vigil lamp burned in front of a small statue of Madonna and Child: it felt like a gesture of farewell. Most of the oil in the lamp had burned, which meant that it had been lit some time ago. The Mother Superior then knew that she had arrived too late.

She walked with a lamp to the car shed, where she was surprised to find that Beatriz had taken the donkey instead of the Ford. But the car was useless: its tyres were slashed and its engine damaged in a way that could only be repaired with parts brought from the city. For a moment Sister María Inés did not understand why the nun had chosen not to drive away in the car. Then she guessed that if Sister Beatriz had left the animal behind one might still get to the city and raise the alarm. Now, of course, the nuns were completely cut off from the world and had to wait for someone to come. Under the car was a pool of lubricant, and Sister María Inés knelt down with the lamp to inspect the damage. She regretted having taught her protégé how to service the car: she could not refill the engine with oil because the plug of the sump was missing. She shone the lamp into every corner of the shed and her despair grew. It was impossible to go after the woman and child in the night. She did not even have an idea which direction they might have taken.

When she came out of the shed, she was still inconsolable but somehow no longer surprised by what had happened. It felt like a prophecy she had pretended to ignore but had nevertheless come true. Her breath was white in the night air. She worried about the child being out on such a cold night. The scant moonlight did not reach under the arches of the cloister as she walked back to the dormitory. She tried to remember whether Beatriz had ever done anything that could have warned her about this but came up with nothing. She thought: 'What will happen to me now?' If it was another test of her faith and ability to serve God, she had failed it. Perhaps, even, the coming of the child was never meant to be a chance to redeem herself but was part of her never-ending punishment. Either way, it was clear to her now that she was damned to perdition.

She did not understand why Beatriz, her favourite nun, would steal the child. A feeling of hatred grew in her stomach and almost made her vomit, but it abruptly passed. It was difficult to despise her truly: she had exhausted that feeling on Sister Ana. She wondered whether she would ever find Beatriz and realised that she did not even know her real name. The Order did not demand to know anything about the past of its members; they could call themselves whatever they liked and when they took their vows they were given a religious name.

She went back to the young nun's room and searched with great care but little hope. She found no clues that could explain her actions, only the traces of a life neatly and quietly lived. She opened the wardrobe – it was empty. She returned to Sister Ana's room and told the other nuns to leave. Sister Ana gave her an angry look. The Mother Superior said: 'You are responsible for this.'

'I only obey God and the law. Beatriz is as guilty as you are, but at least she is not a lunatic.'

'Why did she take the child?'

'I don't know. She was no friend of mine – she was yours.'

'Is she taking him to the city? To the orphanage?'

Dawn was breaking outside. It was time for prayer but the Mother Superior did not care for that now. She stared at the window and again considered whether she should go after Beatriz and the child.

She admitted to herself that it would be pointless – she would not find them. Suddenly she regretted having poisoned the dogs. They might have been able to pick up the scent of the donkey. She said: 'I was responsible for that child.'

'If it were not for you, the child would now be safe in the orphanage. In any case the matter is settled as far as our convent is concerned. The rest is up to the Guardia. What you did was against the law.'

'Christians should not be troubled about the earthly laws.'

'I always suspected that there was something wrong with you, but I could not quite put my finger on it,' Sister Ana said. 'It seems to me there is something in your past – a crime maybe? You still try to escape from it. Your obsession with the child must be related to it.'

'The child is in danger. They will not make it across the mountains. The cold is terrible at night.'

'Don't worry about them. They will be picked up by the Guardias soon enough.'

'I hope not. For Renato's sake.'

'For the Order's sake,' the other woman said. 'Or else everyone will know what happened here. You would be in trouble with the Guardia too.'

'I did what God wanted me to do,' the Mother Superior said without anger. 'It does not matter what happens to me now.'

The more she thought about the child, the more she believed that the misfortune had little to do with anyone but herself. She knew that other people played a very small part in a predicament that was intended solely for her. She said: 'Everything is lost.'

The bell rang for dawn prayer. 'I am going to the chapel,' Sister Ana said. 'Ask God to forgive you for your madness.'

The Mother Superior waved her away. Something drained

from her soul like blood. Feeling weak, she asked the other woman to lead the prayers that day. She was tired and all she wanted to do was go to bed. The sun already stood above the mountain ridges. She had never before watched the moment after sunrise from the windows of the convent: she had always been in the chapel getting ready for prayer. She thought that there is a multitude of worlds one is not aware of – worlds that are as elusive as the spirit world. Then, one day, something happens . . . She laughed, feeling absurd, and said: 'Excuse me, Sister Ana. I am not feeling well. I have to lie down for a while.' She went to her room, where she lay in bed all morning without falling asleep, in case she had another bad dream like the previous night. Then, just before lunchtime, she heard the van from the orphanage pulling up outside the convent.

It was a long time before normality returned to the convent of Our Lady of Mercy. Sister María Inés mourned the child as intensely as if he had died and she had been responsible for his death. She grieved for the fact that she would never see him again and, at the same time, was full of remorse for having failed to protect him from the powers that conspired against her hope of redemption. It would have eased her pain little to learn that the woman who spirited him away was, in fact, his mother. Sister María Inés would still have insisted that the child was hers and only hers because God, in His infinite wisdom, which no man can grasp, had arranged everything so that she had been given the opportunity to make amends for the sin she had committed in her youth.

She had no doubt that it was so, and also that she would never be given another chance. She took refuge in her room and came out rarely, always when the nuns were in the chapel. She did not go to prayer herself but stayed mostly in bed and had her meals brought to her. She ate very little and was running one of her periodic fevers. Suspecting that her old malaria was returning, she began to take quinine, several tablets a day, which caused her to break out in sweats and suffer headaches and confusion. She endured the effects of the medicine without complaint, without cold compresses, without asking for help, and did not cut down on the pills, because she thought that her suffering was a suitable prelude to her ultimate punishment, which God – or she herself – had yet to come up with.

As soon as the people from the orphanage returned to the city, they notified the Guardia Civil about the disappearance of Sister

Beatriz and the child, but it was another two days before an officer came to the convent to interview the nuns. With even more delay, a unit of Guardias on horseback searched the mountains but found no sign of Sister Beatriz or anyone who had seen her, and after a few weeks the investigation was quietly dropped.

The news of the young nun's disappearance horrified Bishop Estrada. His first thought was that she intended to blackmail him, and he reviewed his finances in anticipation of her demands. None came. Next, he began to fear that she would take revenge by destroying his reputation, and talked to lawyers who advised him to deny everything. When months had passed and still no summons had arrived from the Vatican, he began to believe that he would never hear from Sister Beatriz again. It was time to deal with the situation at the convent of Our Lady of Mercy.

Pledging never to visit again the place where the Devil had ambushed him, he did everything by post. He wrote letters recommending Sister Ana to the post of sister visitatrix, as he had promised her, removed Sister María Inés from the position of mother superior, for having showed poor judgement on the matter of the orphan, and put Sister Teresa in charge. Sister María Inés received her punishment with indifference. She had to give up her spacious room because it was set aside for the use of the mother superior of the time, and did so as soon as she was told. Then she did something that surprised the sisters: instead of one of the vacant rooms in the dormitory, she chose to move to the derelict school for novices.

She had not been inside in a very long time and did not expect it to be in such a bad state, but that did not change her mind. Determined not to let the building impose its will on her, she worked for several weeks to make it fit to live in while sleeping on a mattress on the ground floor. Sister Lucía offered to help her but Sister María Inés wanted to be near no one, be friends with no one, speak to no one: she just wanted them to leave her alone. First, she cleared the rooms of the old furniture and bric-a-brac which over the years had found their way, like flotsam washed up on the shore, to the abandoned building from across the convent: stern mattresses stuffed with wool and horsehair which still preserved the shape of the body that years before had taken its last breath on them, cupboards where the rats had made their nests and innumerable desks, chairs, candlesticks and such-like items left behind from the shipwreck of centuries-old life. Then she plastered and painted the walls, fixed the door hinges and finally replaced the broken glass in the windows to stop herself from freezing to death as the winds blew down from the peaks of the sierra in deep winter.

Out of respect, Sister Teresa did not assign any duties to her until she had finished the repairs to the school for novices. Then she asked her to choose what she wanted to do. Sister María Inés did not have to think before answering: 'The Ford.' She did not want to be the one who drove to the city and bought the supplies, a task that remained with Sister Lucía, only to continue to service the car the way she used to do in happier times. The new Mother Superior was happy to grant her wish: Sister María Inés was the only one who could repair the damage that Sister Beatriz had done to the car. Without it their only contact with the outside world was Father Mateo, who came every Sunday, his mule laden with provisions for the convent.

Over the following months Sister María Inés worked on the Ford with parts ordered from the garage in the city. When the repairs were finished, she went to see the new Mother Superior and asked for an additional duty: to ring the bell that called the nuns to prayer. Impressed by her humility, Sister Teresa granted her that wish too.

Winter came early that year and it was more severe and

prolonged than any the nuns could remember. In February the convent became snowbound for several weeks and the nuns had to cut back on food so that it would last until the road to the city reopened. All that time Sister María Inés had not stopped taking the quinine pills. They still did not cure her fever and tormented her with headaches that blinded her with pain. One morning she woke up trembling with cold because the wind had pushed open an unlatched window. In the confusion of the quinine, she saw something in a shadowy corner of the room. It was the child dressed in the white christening gown she had sewn for him, and he was playing with a rosary. She sat up in bed and watched him with curiosity. Suddenly a voice said from the other end of the room: 'It is time you rang the bell.' She turned and greeted the shadow near the door: 'I have been waiting for you, Beatriz.' The young woman stood with her hands clasped, staring back at her. She did not wear a habit. Sister María Inés said: 'Come closer. Do not be afraid. I am not blaming you. We all make mistakes.' She went back to observing the boy playing quietly with the rosary. Without moving from the door, the young woman said again: 'It is time you rang the bell, Mother.' Sister María Inés remembered that soon it would be time for the dawn prayer. 'Yes. Let me do that, child,' she said. 'I will be right back.' She got out of bed and began to dress. She felt with fear that something was going to happen . . . something over which she had no control. The young woman said in a slow and serious voice: 'We won't be here when you come back.' Sister María Inés asked: 'Why not, child? I'll only be a minute.' Her hands trembled as she put on her habit, her belt, her veil . . . She was in a hurry and could not find her rosary: of course, the child had it. Behind her, Sister Beatriz said firmly: 'No. It'd be better if you didn't come back.' Sister María Inés said: 'Oh, I only want to talk . . . I have no intention . . . A lot has happened since you were gone.' In the corner, the child continued to play with the rosary. Sister María Inés finished dressing and knelt down but the child did not want to give up the rosary. 'You're late,' the young woman said while Sister María Inés gently tried to take the rosary from the child. The moment she succeeded, the string of beads turned into a snake which slithered off her fingers. Tears streamed down her face and for a moment she shut her eyes. When she looked again, neither Beatriz nor the child was there. She searched every room but did not find them and went to ring the bell for dawn prayer . . .

She refused to admit that she was suffering from delusions. It did not seem strange to her that Beatriz would come back to the convent just to speak to her. She began to sleep very little because every noise, every shadow, every current of air blowing through the room made her open her eyes, light the candle and peer into the dark until she was certain that there was no one there. She still carried out her duties, but her mind was full of what Beatriz had told her. She looked for her and the child everywhere, scrutinising the sisters' faces and their every word and action, seized by the suspicion that they were hiding the child from her.

It was some time before she admitted that her behaviour was absurd and thought with horror that she was starting to lose her mind. She immediately stopped taking the quinine pills, which she blamed for her hallucinations, and rid herself of everything that reminded her of the child: the cradle, the blanket, the clothes embroidered with cherubs and sequins. Soon she stopped looking for ghosts and became more peaceful, but still could not stop thinking about what Beatriz had asked her to do that dawn in her room: *Ring the bell and do not come back.*

It became a riddle which at first she interpreted as an instruction to quit the Order and leave the convent. The thought of returning to the outside world filled her with misgivings.

She had been prepared to do it to save the child but now saw no reason for it, and told herself that the words had to mean something else. The riddle bothered her all spring. She would be in the shed working on the car and it would come to mind, and then she would rub her forehead with greasy hands, speaking to herself as if arguing with someone. At other times she would simply sit with her head bowed, deep in thought, unaware of what was happening around her, her open eyes the only sign that she had not fallen asleep. In the chapel she stayed kneeling in silence long after the other sisters had gone, but instead of praying she was again thinking about what Sister Beatriz had told her during the illusory visit. She continued to live in the school for novices. At Sister Teresa's insistence, she had accepted the petrol heater which she had bought for the child, and left it burning near her bed all night. Her only true company were the ghosts that haunted the derelict building. Every night she heard the empty rooms echo with voices that repeated the catechism. In the morning the blackboards were filled with conjugations of Latin verbs. One day she discovered a scroll of parchment in the scriptorium on which someone had copied in a beautiful hand, and with ink that was still wet, the poems of Teresa of Ávila: *Give me wealth or want, delight or distress, happiness or gloominess, Heaven or Hell, sweet life, sun unveiled, to You I give all.* She was terrified to think that she might have left her bed in the middle of the night and done all this herself but in the morning could not remember it. And so she began to go from room to room sweeping the floors, fixing the locks, hammering nails, doing all sorts of odd jobs that did not need to be done but kept her busy, which was her simple tactic in her battle against madness.

One day, while replacing the glass in a window broken by the wind, she cut herself badly. She looked at the blood on her fingers and at that moment the answer to the riddle that had been troubling her for months came to her at last. Leaving drops of blood behind her on the floor, she returned to her room, where instead of treating her cuts she sat on the bed and began to say the rosary: '*Ave Maria, gratia plena, Dominus tecum . . .*'

She did not decide what to do right away. She deliberated on the matter all summer, coming up with sound reasons for and against her decision, changing her mind several times, until she ran out of arguments and counter-arguments and simply went through the motions, knowing that she was set on doing what she had decided to do. She chose a day and thought that she would do it at dawn, but when the time came she changed her mind with the excuse that she should attend prayers one last time. Then, just before the early morning prayer, Sister Teresa came to her room simply to see how she was, and walked with her to the chapel when it was time to ring the bell. At the next prayer of the day her hands were so weak and she trembled so much that she could hardly ring the bell. Finally, three further hours later, when the clock on the bell tower said almost midday, she felt that she was ready.

She had gone through it many times, and what she had to do was as clear and precise as the ritual of Mass. She took her rosary from her belt and kissed it, but there was no time to say a prayer. She placed it on her bed and took off her belt and placed it next to it. Then she took off her veil and the rest of her habit except for her white tunic, folding each item neatly and placing it on the bed. While she did all that, slowly and methodically, she began to recall everything that had happened since the summer of the previous year. She remembered when she had woken up and found the cradle empty, then the attack of the dog in the courtyard and then the day when on the steps of the convent she had taken the child out of the old suitcase. Then she discovered, to her dismay, that she could no longer remember his face:

they could show her any baby and she would believe he was Renato. If she had not failed in her duty, she would have lived to see him grow into someone she could remember.

But she had no time to dwell on what could have been. She only said: 'Dear God, keep him safe,' as if waving goodbye to someone from a train that has begun to move. The rest of her past came to her, her memory growing clearer the further back it travelled. She remembered her time as a missionary nurse in Africa, where she had secretly hoped to catch a disease and die like a saint, not knowing that God had other designs on her. Before leaving her room, she also relived the moment when she had heard the news of her fiancé's death, the visit to the woman in another town and the end of her pregnancy in a small room of a beautiful villa. Her last memory was of making love for the first and last time in her life, which she still associated with the smell of blood.

She came out of the school for novices in only her thin tunic and began to shiver despite the warm weather. A nun filling buckets at the well did not raise her head. Sister María Inés went quickly to the chapel and climbed the steps to the top of the bell tower. She gathered the rope of the bell that reached the ground and looped a noose around her neck. Then the enormity of what she was about to do hit her, and she hesitated. But she wanted to do it. She said: 'Don't be afraid. I'm not killing you but the evil that lives inside you independently of your will. It's not a sin to cast out a demon.' As if to support her argument, she began to recite the prayer of exorcism. A few precious minutes of life went by. She raised her head and looked at the pine forest and the mountains beyond. From where she stood she could also see the cemetery. She knew that she would not be buried there because the Church considered what she was about to do a mortal sin. She was about to step into the void when she saw somebody riding an animal along the road. She could not help but believe that it was Beatriz coming back with the child, and she would not have to go through with her plan. But soon she saw that it was only Father Mateo on his mule. Her heart sank with this final disappointment and she crossed herself. It was time.

A long drop, a current of cold air and the heavy pull of the rope: light went out but she could still hear the tolling of the bell, first on its own, then mixed with screaming voices. Was it possible that she could hear all that? For a moment her heart beat with the hope of eternal life: she had been forgiven at the last moment. But then the bell slowly stopped tolling, the rope became tighter around her neck and she felt weightless like a feather. With the last drop of her senses, she could tell that *now* was, in fact, the instant when one passed through the threshold and joined the legion of souls, good and bad alike, which roamed blindly in the dark no longer plagued by memory.

Father Mateo had heard the tolling of the bell but not the screams when, a little while later, he knocked on the door of the convent.

Despite its load and the difficult terrain, the animal climbed the slope without a pause, putting down its hooves in the gaps between the jagged rocks, which were wet and slippery. It had been raining all morning but Sister Beatriz had pushed on out of fear that they might be coming after her. She sat astride the donkey, holding the saddle and covered with a large piece of canvas that fell over her body and the baby, who was cradled in the sling tied to her front. The rain soaked the thick canvas and dripped down Midas's back. Over her habit she wore her coat but it was very thin and she still shivered with cold. She did not wear her veil but a straw hat that was no good against the wind and the rain. She had followed no trail as often as she could, cutting across the forested slopes to make it harder for whoever pursued her to track her.

When she had gone to see Sister María Inés in her room to discuss the Bishop's decision to give the child to the orphanage, Sister Beatriz had been surprised to hear the Mother Superior deny the bad news. The way the Bishop had spoken to Sister Beatriz in their meeting earlier that day, the tone of his voice, his detailed plans for the future of the child, his promise to look after him as long as she gave him up, had convinced the young woman that the Mother Superior had not been telling her the truth. So Sister Beatriz had observed her carefully, pretending to listen to her reassurances and trying to hide her mistrust, until she had figured out that the Mother Superior had been planning to run away from the convent with the child. Sister Beatriz had returned to her room and quickly decided to act.

They left the pine forest behind and began to cross a large

plateau of red earth and rock surrounded in all directions by the peaks of the sierra. Travelling slowly across the barren stretch of land, she felt tired and lonely. Even a solitary bird of prey now circling in the sky made her fear that it might lead her pursuers to her. When she reached the edge of the plateau, she stopped and looked back in the direction she had come from; she saw no one following her. She told herself that it was unreasonable to expect that they would: the sisters could neither come after her on foot nor go to the city and call for help. She had made sure the damage to the Ford was impossible to repair with the tools at the convent. The thought calmed her down and she looked for somewhere to rest. At an abandoned mine she left Midas to chew at a thorn bush while she and the baby sheltered from the rain inside. The darkness of the mineshaft unnerved her. She took off her canvas cloak and stood listening to the rain a few steps from the entrance. Although the child was asleep, she unbuttoned her coat and, shivering, gave him her breast. He was used to it and began to feed without opening his eyes.

Outside, the rain tapped against the trees and the fallen leaves. After years in the daily company of the other nuns, she was now alone in the world. The ancient walls of the convent had protected her from the influenza epidemic but failed to save her from the machinations of love. The child came off the breast and she covered herself, put him in the sling and mounted Midas again. The rain had stopped when they entered an oak forest and began to climb once more. At the top of the highest crest, she stopped and studied the valley ahead dotted with villages, then pushed the animal in the direction of the village that was not closest but easiest to get to. Some time later she came to the first farmhouses and dogs came barking. She ignored them – she was more afraid of people and the Guardia Civil. She continued towards the pointed roof of the bell tower in the middle of the village. Somebody came to the door of a house and she greeted him casually, but he stared at her, saying nothing. In the square she got off the donkey and led him to a fountain where a mule was also drinking. Then she entered the church to rest and decide what to do away from the villagers' stares.

She felt good in the bare, dark church that reminded her of the chapel in the convent. She placed the child on a pew and knelt down to pray. As soon as she had finished and made the sign of the Cross, a voice behind her said: 'Excuse me. I believe we have met.' She turned and saw Father Mateo standing a few feet away with his hands clasped inside the sleeves of his cassock. He added: 'I'm afraid I can't recall where.'

Sister Beatriz said: 'No, Father. I don't think—'

'Ah yes,' the young priest said. 'The convent – isn't that right? You're not wearing your veil, Sister. Is anything the matter? I'm afraid I've forgotten your name.'

She thought quickly what to do. 'I am sorry, Father. I didn't recognise you,' she said. 'I didn't know this was your parish.'

'Oh no. I have no parish. The local priest has fallen ill. They send me wherever I'm needed.' He looked with uncertain eyes at the child sleeping on the pew.

'This is Renato,' the woman said. 'The child you baptised.'

'I don't understand.'

Sister Beatriz took the child in her arms and asked: 'Will you hear my confession, Father?'

'Of course, Sister. Do you want us to do it now?'

He turned towards the confessional but she touched his arm. 'We can do it right here, can't we, Father? No one knows me in this place.'

'Yes, by all means. The box is not essential.'

'You're very kind, Father.' She unbuttoned her coat and saw that the young man looked at her white habit with a kind of relief. She said: 'I'm no longer a nun, Father.'

'What happened?'

Instead of answering him she began: 'Bless me Father for I have sinned,' and he immediately understood that she would talk to him only if he promised to reveal nothing. 'Please go on, Sister,' he said. 'It is forbidden for a confessor to betray a penitent in any way and for any reason.'

She smiled at his solemnity, which was unusual for someone of his age, and felt reassured that she could trust him. Then, in a low but unfaltering voice, she told him about the child from the moment of his birth until now, talking in great detail about everything but without ever mentioning the Bishop.

'This is a very serious matter,' Father Mateo said when she finished.

'I'm ashamed of breaking my vows,' Sister Beatriz said. 'But I regret nothing that I did once I discovered I was pregnant.'

'Yes. I understand, of course . . . And the father?'

'The father has nothing to do with it,' the woman said sharply. The priest blushed. 'Oh, I didn't mean . . . I'm not interested in gossip. If you thought that . . . I apologise.' He quickly absolved her and asked her to recite an act of contrition.

When Sister Beatriz finished, she said: 'Now I need your help with a practical matter, Father.'

'My help? I prefer not to get involved with something that—'

'I need clothes.'

'Oh, I see. There is a woman who cleans the church once a week. Perhaps she leaves her work clothes here.' He led the way to the storeroom, where they found an old dress. The priest said: 'I'm afraid it's not very clean and certainly not warm enough for this weather.'

'It'll do. I have a coat. It's only for another day or two, Father – until I get to a place where I can buy proper clothes.'

He nodded, looking constantly at the door, afraid that someone might come and find them together in the storeroom. He walked out to let her change. A moment later she reappeared wearing the old dress and carrying the child in the sling. The priest felt awkward at her transformation: she was a pretty woman. She looked at him and said with a smile: 'God has sent you to us, Father Mateo.'

'I hope that you know what you're doing, Sister.'

'Please take this,' she said and gave him the habit.

He looked at it, not knowing what to do with it.

Sister Beatriz said: 'I think you should burn it.'

'No. It isn't right.'

She shrugged. 'As you wish.' She opened her purse and offered him a few coins. 'For the cleaning lady – to pay for the dress.'

The priest took the money. He tried to think of something to say but came up with nothing. The seminary had not prepared him for a situation like this one. He was guided only by his conscience and the instinct to do good. Sister Beatriz asked: 'Is there any quick way to get to a big town on this side of the mountains?'

Father Mateo checked his watch. 'There is a bus,' he said. 'But not for a while. Are you being followed?'

'No. I took care of that.'

He calmed down a little. 'Ah good, good. And the animal?'

'Midas? Find a home for him – someone who won't work him hard.'

They sat near the door to wait for the bus. Sister Beatriz stroked the child in his sling and looked round. It was one of those poor churches built by the community itself, with unadorned whitewashed walls, simple benches for pews and an altar made of wood. She felt safe and calm, as if it were a sanctuary for both her body and soul. She had travelled a long way from the convent of Our Lady of Mercy in a day, much further than she had expected. Suddenly she lost her nerve. She told herself that she would do anything to go back, promise everything, ask forgiveness. She thought that she could simply hand the child over to the young priest with the words: 'Do what you want with him.' But whatever she felt only lasted a moment. Saying nothing, she took the child from his sling and cradled him in her arms.

There were footsteps outside, and a boy came to the door. The priest looked at him: 'What is it?'

'Sir, my mother asks whether you'll say Mass this evening.'

'I will.'

'And whether she could take communion.'

'Has she been fasting from food and drink all day?'

'No, sir.'

'Is she sick?'

'No.'

'Then she can't.'

The boy stared at him sullenly for a moment and then went away. Father Mateo looked at his watch again. He said: 'Just a little longer,' and tapped his foot nervously. 'The bus is usually on time. It only stays for a moment.'

'Do we have to go outside?'

'No. We'll hear it from in here.'

'Are there many stops from here to the town?'

'Only a few.'

Sister Beatriz wanted to kiss his hand with gratitude, but he was much younger than her, too young in fact to be used to reverence, and she would probably embarrass him. 'Well, Father,' she said, 'would you like to hold him?'

He looked at the child fearfully. 'Oh no, Sister, thank you. I shouldn't—'

'Only a moment, Father. Please, I'm a little tired.'

'Oh yes, in that case . . .'

He took the child with uncertain hands and sat stiffly on the pew.

'Not like that, Father,' the woman said. 'Like this.' And she placed the child more securely in his arms.

'Ah, I see.'

The woman stared at the man holding the child for a while. Then she said: 'What are you thinking, Father?'

'Oh, nothing. Just that . . . It's strange how a sin . . . a mistake . . . could lead to something so good and innocent.' Father Mateo made an attempt to rock the child but Renato protested and he quickly stopped. 'Perhaps I'm a bad priest. I see nothing evil in this poor child – or in you,' he said and went crimson again. 'Do you have money?'

'I'll be fine, Father.'

'Please don't worry. I'll tell no one – not even His Excellency. It's the Seal of the Confessional.'

'Thank you.'

Sister Beatriz stood up and went to the door. It was afternoon and the air was warmer, but she was glad that she would not have to travel on the animal any more. There was a train station in the town where the bus went. She thought of the Mother Superior and what she would do now that she had lost the child. But he was not her child and she would simply have to go back to her old life. When they heard the bus coming, Father Mateo jumped to his feet and held the child meekly out to her. Then he followed her out to the square, where a few people were already boarding the bus.

'You're a good man, Father,' Sister Beatriz said.

'Oh, I don't know. I try to do what a priest . . . It comes with the territory, doesn't it?'

'Not always.'

Sister Beatriz waited her turn to board the bus. The priest said: 'One more thing, Sister, if I may.'

'What is it?'

'The Mother Superior – I am right in thinking that she was very fond of Renato, isn't that so? God knows how she must be feeling now . . . I think if she knew the truth it would help her.'

'Do you want me to write to her?'

'Would you, Sister? If you please. Make her see the way things turned out is for the best.'

'I don't know. What if—'

'Oh, not now. After you have settled down. Post the letter in another town not where you live. That way it'll be impossible to track you down.'

'Let me think about it, Father.'

She climbed onto the bus and took a window seat, from where she watched the kind young priest waiting humbly with his hands inside the pockets of his cassock. Watching him, she thought again about Sister María Inés and how grateful she ought to be to her. All of a sudden she stood up from her seat and opened the window. She spoke up: 'Tell the Mother that as soon as I have—' But the driver had already shut the door and the rest of what she said was lost in the noise of the engine and the cloud of exhaust in which the priest also vanished.